THE MISSING MAN

"As many of you die-hard fans know, today is a very special occasion," Myra Manning said. "Emory Rex does not like to be seen in public. He does not do book signings. He does not go on publicity tours. He does not do appearances. But today, he's going to grace this very stage to read the conclusion of his new novel, *Murdernet.*"

"If *you* ever get off the stage," Alex grumbled.

"I know you're all eager to see him. So now, without further ado, I present to you . . . Emory Rex!"

She gave a flourish with her arm and tugged on a long, golden, braided rope. The curtains swished open, revealing a wooden chair, a microphone, and a little table with a pitcher of water and a glass.

Then there was a gasp from Myra Manning—and the entire audience.

There was nobody on the stage.

JOIN THE TEAM!

Do you watch GHOSTWRITER on PBS? Then you know that when you read and write to solve a mystery or unravel a puzzle, you're using the same smarts and skills the Ghostwriter Team uses.

We hope you'll join the team and read along to help solve the mysterious and puzzling goings-on in all of the GHOSTWRITER books!

the man who vanished

by Amy Keyishian

illustrated by Michael David Biegel

A Children's Television Workshop Book

Bantam Books
New York   Toronto   London
Sydney   Auckland

THE MAN WHO VANISHED
A Bantam Book / June 1996

Cover design by Marietta Anastassatos
Cover photo of chair © 1996 Will Ryan.

ISBN 0-553-48398-6

Published simultaneously in the United States and Canada

Bantam Books are published by Bantam Books, a division of Bantam Doubleday Dell Publishing Group, Inc. Its trademark, consisting of the words "Bantam Books" and the portrayal of a rooster, is registered in U.S. Patent and Trademark Office and in other countries. Marca Registrada. Bantam Books, 1540 Broadway, New York, New York 10036.

PRINTED IN THE UNITED STATES OF AMERICA

OPM   0 9 8 7 6 5 4 3 2

the man who vanished

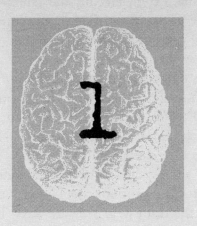

His heart pounding, Eric Moseby stared at the huge steel door. He could feel sweat rolling down his face, and his hands were trembling. Behind him, guards from the computer company were closing in. In front of him was the secret at the center of the huge computer network. He had to disconnect the power source and destroy the computer's massive memory banks before the guards got there.

Moseby pushed through the cold steel door. Something was wrong. At the center of a computer network this large, there should have been a huge, humming machine. But the room was almost empty. And all he heard was an ominous silence.

Alex Fernandez stopped reading and looked up at his friends. Most of the members of the Ghostwriter

Team—Tina, Lenni, Hector, and Jamal—were sitting in the Fernandezes' bodega, listening to Alex read the story from a horror magazine.

It was a sweltering day in the middle of the hottest Brooklyn summer on record. There were two giant fans set up in the little grocery store, and everyone had a cold drink. But it didn't seem to help. The store still felt like an oven, and the air was so humid, Alex felt as if he needed gills to breathe.

Still, he was psyched to have his friends around.

Summertime meant no school—but it also meant that often the team went separate ways. Lenni Frazier, who was twelve, usually went to a music day camp, and Jamal Jenkins, who was thirteen, studied karate. They both had the day off today, though, and they were tossing a tennis ball back and forth as they sat on the floor of the bodega.

Nine-year-old Hector Carrero was also there. Hector helped out a lot in the Fernandezes' store during the summer. Alex was his "big brother"—he helped Hector with his schoolwork and hung out with him because Hector's dad wasn't around.

Tina was there, too. Tina was good friends with Alex's little sister, Gaby. But to Alex, Tina was more than just his bratty sister's sidekick. He almost couldn't tell that Tina was only eleven. Alex fought with Gaby a lot—Tina seemed to have so much more common sense. He liked spending time with her.

In fact, Tina was the one who had suggested that Alex read this horror story out loud to the rest of the team. She thought it would help everyone forget about the heat. Tina loved horror stories. And she looked as if she was really enjoying this one.

The only ones missing were Gaby and Jamal's cousin Casey. They were spending the week at summer camp—probably splashing around in some cool blue lake.

Alex wiped the sweat from his face and took a long gulp of ice-cold water. He was about to continue reading when he saw an eerie green glow lighting up words in the magazine. It was Ghostwriter, the team's invisible friend who helped them solve mysteries.

Ghostwriter could not talk or hear, but he could read words anywhere—even in a closed book or on a computer. He could also take letters from different places and spell out messages for the team. Often Ghostwriter could sense how the team was feeling.

Nobody was really sure what—or who—Ghostwriter was. Only the kids on the Ghostwriter Team could see him. All they knew was he was definitely their friend.

Alex watched Ghostwriter read the words on the page. He was wondering if his friend was enjoying the story when a voice broke into his thoughts.

"Hellooo!" Alex looked up and saw Tina smiling at him from her metal folding chair, right next to the Alpo and the Kitty Litter for sale in the store. "Well?" she said. "Come on, Alex! What happens next? What's in the big room at the center of the computer complex?"

"Ugh, who cares?" Lenni said, tugging her long brown hair into a ponytail and holding a cold soda can against the back of her neck.

"What's the matter, Lenni? You don't like the story?" Alex asked. The story was by his absolute favorite author, Emory Rex.

"These horror stories are so dumb," Lenni said.

"Lenni, this isn't just any horror story. This is Emory Rex!" Alex insisted. "He puts out a new book practically every year, and it's always on the best-seller list."

"So what?" Lenni said. "Just because a book sells a lot, that doesn't make it good. This story doesn't make any sense at all. I don't get what's going on."

Alex sighed. "I told you. Emory Rex's new book has been coming out, chapter by chapter, in the magazine *Gotham City Horror Chronicles*. The story is about a lonely guy, a computer programmer, who leaves his regular job to go work for this big mysterious corporation on a Caribbean island. But when he gets there—"

"I know, I know," Lenni interrupted, waving her hands to stop him. "He gets to this strange new job, and they tell him to design a super virtual-reality world that would never fit in the memory of a regular computer. And he falls in love with this woman, Janet, but she disappears and he has to go looking for her. And that's when he finds his way into the computer complex."

"Yeah!" Hector said. He was sitting on the freezer case. "Maybe there are computer ninjas in there and they're going to battle! *Bam! POW!*" He imitated some karate moves. "I like this story. Read some more, Alex!"

Alex looked down at the magazine and tried to find his place again. "Okay, let's see," he said.

And all he heard was an ominous silence.

"You read that already!" Hector complained. "And what's *ominous* mean, anyway?"

"It means, like, creepy and spooky. Like when he heard that silence, he just knew something was wrong," Alex said.

"Oh, okay. You can keep reading," Hector announced with a wave of his hand.

"Thanks, Hector," Alex said, rolling his eyes.

Where were the controls? Where was the power? Moseby felt sick with disgust when he saw what was at the center of the most powerful computer in the world: A human brain.

Wires came from all corners of the room and hooked up to the small, wrinkly, wet object. It was pulsating with the effort of keeping the massive network running. It was dark and rotten at the edges, almost like a dying flower. No wonder the computer was breaking down. This brain looked as if it was ready to collapse.

Moseby dropped to his knees and gagged. Before he could back out the door, he heard clattering footsteps behind him. There was no escape now.

He crawled behind a clump of wires, hoping for a few seconds to think of what to do next.

But it wasn't the guards who burst through the door. It was the evil Dr. Picket. And he had Janet—strapped to a bed with wheels.

"Don't struggle, my sweet little pretty," Dr. Picket cooed. "It will all be over soon. And I need your brain in perfect condition."

"Eeeeeeeeeeewwwwww!" Everybody groaned in disgust.

"That's exactly what I mean," Lenni said. "What's so great about that? It's totally disgusting. That's not writing! It's vomiting on paper!"

"Come on! It's fun to read," Alex said. "Right, Jamal?"

Jamal was sitting directly in front of one of the fans, letting the breeze blow the sweat off him. "Um . . . well, actually, Alex," he said sheepishly, "I kind of agree with Lenni."

"You do?" Alex threw his hands in the air. "I give up! You mean you don't like this story either?"

"Well, it's fun to listen to . . . but it's kind of stupid," Jamal explained. "And all of Emory Rex's books are sort of the same. You know something bad will happen, but the good guy will win in the end. And in between, there's going to be a lot of gross stuff."

"And this story is a perfect example," Lenni said. "The hero—this guy Moseby—well, he could tell the computer complex was dangerous as soon as he got to the job. He saw the soldiers guarding it! So why didn't he just leave? Nobody told him to go poking his nose into everything."

"But his girlfriend disappeared," Hector said. "He's got to go rescue her!"

Lenni rolled her eyes. "Oh, spare me," she moaned. "*Rescue* her? That's another problem with these dumb horror books. All the girls in them end up twisting their ankles and screaming for help."

"Lenni, I think you're being too hard on Emory Rex," Tina said. "I agree with you that the female characters in his books could be better—but he tells stories really well. You just can't take them too seriously."

Alex grinned at Tina gratefully. Somehow she always managed to stop an argument before it started, without making anyone feel bad.

"Yeah! Don't take them so seriously," Hector said. "I love Emory Rex. Especially when they make movies of his books. Remember *My Body, My Enemy*? It was totally sick!"

"You mean the one about the guy whose guts start taking over his body?" Jamal asked.

"Oh, come on," Lenni moaned. "That's not even possible."

"It may not be possible, but it happened to the guy in this movie," Hector continued. "His internal organs started taking over the rest of his body. And they started battling against each other—his pancreas wanted to rule, and so did his kidneys. Finally his stomach made a move."

Hector stood up and held his hands out, setting the scene. His brown eyes were shining. "He was sitting there in the laboratory, where they were studying what was happening to him, right? Because nobody could figure it out. And all of a sudden— *Bam! Crunch! Squish!* His stomach punches a hole in his abdomen and munches its way out, and it *eats* the rest of him. Like, it totally devours him!" He shuddered, but he was also smiling. "It was disgusting."

"Greeeat," Lenni said. "Disgusting is just *great.*"

"I wish you would all stop reading those stupid books," Mrs. Fernandez called out from the back of the bodega, where she was sorting mangoes. "Alex had such terrible nightmares after the last one he read. What was it called? *Department Store Death*?"

"It was called *Bloomingdeath*," Alex said grumpily. "And I did not have nightmares."

"You did so!" Mrs. Fernandez insisted. "You were scared that the mannequins in the windows would really come to life. I couldn't get you to go Christmas shopping with me!"

Alex's face turned red. Lenni was about to start teasing him when Tina cut her off.

"I was scared too," Tina admitted. "My mom was mad at me because I wouldn't eat anything with noodles in it for months. They reminded me of intestines!"

Everybody laughed. Alex smiled gratefully at Tina again.

"Huh! Speak of the devil," Mr. Fernandez said.

He was sitting behind the counter, reading the newspaper.

"Is that the name of the new Emory Rex novel?" Jamal cracked.

"No, it's just an expression," Mr. Fernandez said. "I mean, you kids were talking about Emory Rex, and right here in the paper there's an announcement about him."

"Really? What does it say?" Alex demanded. Mr. Fernandez held up the paper and showed them the headline:

EMORY REX TO READ AT HORROR CONVENTION

Tina let out a shriek, and Alex was across the store in a flash. The words pulsated with a green light as Ghostwriter read them too.

"He's going to be at a convention for horror-book fans," Alex shouted as he read the article. "And he's going to read the end of *Murdernet!*"

"You mean the story you were just reading to us from the magazine?" Tina said. "We're finally going to hear how it ends?"

"I don't get it," Hector said, looking confused. "They've been publishing a chapter of that book each month. Aren't they going to have the last chapter too?"

"I guess not," Alex said. "It says here that the only way to find out the ending before the actual book

comes out is to come to the convention and hear Emory Rex read it."

"You guys, we've *got* to go to this convention!" Tina announced.

"Count me out," Lenni said. "You know how I feel about Emory Rex."

"I'm not really interested either," Jamal said. "Sorry, guys."

"Oh, no!" Hector groaned. "It's the same day as the YMCA trip to Splashland. My mom already paid for it—and I really want to go. I'm going to miss the convention too!"

"I guess it's just you and me, Alex," Tina said. "I'm not about to let you hear the end of the story without me."

"Really?" Alex felt a flush of excitement. "So we're going?" He looked at his father. "We're allowed to go?"

Mrs. Fernandez was walking to the front of the store, wiping her hands. She and her husband exchanged glances, and Mrs. Fernandez shrugged.

"All right," Mr. Fernandez said. "Yes, you can go, if the two of you are going together. But no nightmares!"

"Nightmares? Are you kidding?" Alex said. "This is a dream come true. I'm going to see Emory Rex!"

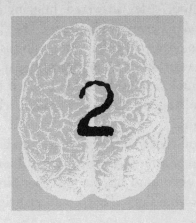

A week later Alex and Tina were riding the subway train, hurtling toward Manhattan in an underground tunnel. It was still sweltering hot outside—but inside the train it was freezing, thanks to the supercool air-conditioning.

Alex stared across the car at the big red circle with a 2 in the middle. He knew the number two train would take them to the hotel where the convention was. But he couldn't help feeling nervous. It wasn't every day that Alex traveled on the subway with another kid—and no grown-ups. He felt excited and important, but a little bit scared, too.

There was no way he was going to admit that to Tina. She looked cool as a cucumber. She'd think he was a total geek if she knew how nervous he was. Tina grinned at Alex and tapped the copy of Emory Rex's book *Bloomingdeath* on her lap.

"All ready for signing," she said.

"Mine too," Alex answered, hugging his copy of *My Body, My Enemy* to his chest. "They'll be collector's items once we get his autograph inside. I'll bet they'll be worth a lot of money someday."

Tina shook her head. "I don't care if it's worth a million dollars," she said. "I wouldn't sell this book for anything."

The train clattered along, then screeched to a halt at Chambers Street. Just before the doors closed, a woman rushed onto the train. She sat directly across from Alex and Tina. They couldn't help staring at her.

She had frizzy red hair that sprang out from her head in all directions. Her face was round and pale as the moon. Huge, thick glasses magnified her watery blue eyes. Her lips were decorated with frosty pink lipstick. She kept peering around the car, wrinkling her nose like a rabbit and sniffling.

Suddenly her eyes met Alex's.

"I was in a car that wasn't air-conditioned," she said in a wispy, childlike voice. "I just had to switch."

Alex smiled politely and looked away. When he looked back, she was staring at an advertisement on the wall above his head. He couldn't help looking at the rest of her.

She was wearing a black T-shirt with the words MY BODY, MY ENEMY printed on it. It had a very realistic picture of a stomach that looked as if it was bursting through the shirt, just like in Emory Rex's

book. She was also wearing a flowery cotton skirt, white socks, and brown sandals. Alex noticed that Tina was staring at her too.

"She must be on her way to the horror convention," he whispered to Tina. "That's an awesome T-shirt."

Tina nodded. "But she looks kind of strange," she whispered back.

"You mean her clothes?" Alex asked, grimacing. "She looks like she got dressed during an earthquake. Totally haphazard."

But Tina shook her head. "No, it's not her clothes," she said. "It's that weird, haunted look in her eyes. I hope everyone at the convention isn't like that."

Alex was about to say something about horror fans when the train shuddered, slowed down, and then came to a jolting stop. The lights flickered off, and the fans stopped humming. The car was plunged into total darkness and silence.

It wasn't unusual for the train to stop like that. In fact, it happened all the time, when there was a train on the track ahead. And the lights often went out. It wasn't that big a deal.

Except that Alex was already feeling nervous. His heart was beating so loudly, he was afraid Tina could hear it. He gulped, then concentrated on breathing in and out normally.

"Are you still there?" Tina asked in a small voice. That made Alex feel better. She sounded just as nervous as he was.

"You bet," he said. He reached his hand out for hers and gave it a squeeze. Tina squeezed back, and he felt a bit braver.

Then he had a horrible thought.

Sometimes Alex wished he could switch off his imagination. Once his mind got rolling on something—especially something scary—it was almost impossible to make it stop. This was one of those times.

He could feel Tina's hand in his. At least, he *thought* it was Tina's hand. But what if someone—or some*thing*—had snuck between them when the lights went out? It was pitch black in the car. What if the lights came on and Alex looked next to him, and instead of Tina there was a huge psychopathic murderer with very small hands?

That's probably the stupidest thing you've ever come up with, Alex Fernandez, he said sternly. But he couldn't help imagining what a guy like that would look like. And it wasn't a pretty picture.

"Tina?" he asked, his voice sounding hollow in the silent, cavernous car.

"Yeah?" Tina answered, and Alex felt a flood of relief.

"Nothing," he said, squeezing her hand again. "I just wanted to make sure . . . you know, you were okay."

"I'm okay." She sighed. "I wish I could stop thinking about the alligators, though."

"Oh, no!" With a rush Alex remembered the Emory Rex story about mutated alligators that crawled around in the sewers. They found their way into the subway system of New York. And feasted on human flesh. "I wish you hadn't reminded me of that!" Alex groaned.

As if in response, a thin, reedy voice cut through the inky black silence of the subway car. At first Alex didn't know if it was squeaky machinery or a moaning wind. It was a high-pitched sound, nasal and whiny.

Then he realized someone was actually singing in the pitch-black subway car. And it wasn't normal singing, with a beat and words. It was just a tuneless hum-singing. Alex felt the hair on the back of his neck stand up, and Tina grabbed his hand again—tightly.

"Hmmmmmmm, mmmmmmmm, mmmmmmmmm, hummmmmmmm . . ." The eerie humming continued. Alex wanted to jam his fingers into his ears, only he couldn't. Tina was squeezing his fingers, and he was trying to squeeze back reassuringly, which was hard since she was practically cutting off his circulation.

The train jerked violently and started moving again. The lights flickered on, and Alex and Tina could finally see who was singing. It was the weird woman with the Emory Rex T-shirt. She caught their gaze and gave them a toothy grin.

"I was thinking of the alligators too. But singing always makes me feel less nervous," she said.

Tina and Alex grinned back, but they were both

thinking the same thing. "*Her* singing made me *more* nervous!" Alex whispered under his breath.

There weren't any more delays. Ten minutes later the train arrived at Thirty-fourth Street—Alex and Tina's stop.

The strange woman stood up and walked out of the car sedately, humming to herself in that strange, reedy voice. Alex and Tina were much more excited. They couldn't wait to get off the train and into the convention. They tore through the hallways of the humid station, leaving the woman way behind. They leaped up the stairs two at a time and finally burst into the blazing sunlight of the street.

Splat!

Just in time to see a human body land right in front of them on the concrete sidewalk.

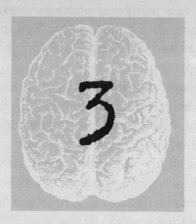

3

Alex let out a startled yelp, and Tina gasped.
They both jumped back and stared at the
ground in front of them. Blood was spreading along
the sidewalk, surrounding the man's body and ooz-
ing toward them. In another few seconds the blood
would stain Alex's black-and-white sneakers, but he
felt as if he were rooted to the pavement.

Slowly it dawned on Alex that the people around
him weren't screaming. They weren't even horrified.
He looked at Tina, but she didn't seem to understand what was happening any better than he did.

"Fools. Fools!" A voice shrieked from an amplifier
behind them, making them jump again. They looked
up, and Tina let out a groan.

"I can't believe I got scared by that," she said.

A young man with curly blond hair and a top hat
was standing on a platform, speaking into a micro-

phone and pointing at a scaffold high up on the building. Everybody was watching him and laughing. Alex took a closer look at the body on the ground. It was a dummy!

"Do you think you can end the life of Jack the Ripper so easily?" the man in the top hat bellowed. "Do you think a ten-story plummet will stop the man who has been keeping London in the icy grip of fear for over a century? Laugh now," he warned, pointing at the body. "But he'll be back. *He'll be back!*"

The man let out a long, demented cackle. Alex knelt down and poked at the plastic skin of the dummy. "Eew! It's clammy and cold," he said, laughing. "You touch it!"

"No way!" Tina said, backing up.

"What's the matter? You scared?" Alex asked teasingly.

"No!" Tina said. "I just want to get to the convention before you do." She raced away from him, toward the door of the hotel.

"Hey!" Alex stumbled as he tried to stand up and almost slipped in the fake blood. "No fair. Wait up!"

He caught up with Tina at the entrance to the main convention hall. The doorway had fake gray stonework all around it. A table set up outside the entrance was draped in black fabric.

"Not scared, huh?" Alex asked.

Tina smirked at him. "Alex, I have better things to do with my time than poke plastic dead guys."

Alex nodded. "Yep. You were terrified."

Tina rolled her eyes and handed her ticket to the woman sitting at the table. She had jet black hair with a white streak in it; her hair was piled high on her head. Her black shirt and skirt were so tight, they looked as if they were painted onto her body. Her lipstick was the color of dried blood.

"Welcome to the horror convention," she said in a deep, breathy voice as she took their tickets. "You'll have to wear these today." She handed them each a nametag. Along the top, printed in black letters that looked as if they were melting, were the words HORROR CONVENTION. There was a blank space underneath. Alex took a red felt-tip pen and wrote his name on his; Tina started to do the same. As she was writing, something dry and scaly brushed against her hand. She pulled her hand back suddenly and looked up.

The woman had a long, thick, white-and-orange snake draped around her shoulders. Its tail had brushed Tina's hand. Tina gulped and finished writing her name, keeping her eyes on the python the whole time. It made her so nervous, her name ended up looking like this: Tina NgUYEN.

"Now make sure you keep those on," the woman warned. "See? I've got mine on." Her nametag, which said VAMPYRA ELSINORE in red letters, was pinned to a round earring that pierced her belly button.

"How come the nametags are so important?" Alex asked, gulping as he stared at the golden ring.

Vampyra leaned forward and narrowed her black-lined eyes. "Because we need to be able to tell who's human . . . and who's a *visitor from beyond*." Then she gave a hissing laugh and kissed the head of her snake.

Alex and Tina looked at each other, then looked back at Vampyra and smiled. They walked through the door into the convention.

"Weird, huh?" Alex said. "People really get into this stuff."

"It's a little corny," Tina admitted. She looked around her at the other convention-goers. Some of them were in costumes; some were just looking at everything, wide-eyed and excited. "But I like it." She grinned.

"Me too," Alex said. "Boy, if Lenni and Jamal were here, they'd have to keep their opinions to themselves. This place is packed with horror fans!"

The convention room was three stories tall. The roof was made of glass to let the sunlight in. But a lot of the people inside looked as if they hadn't seen the sun in years. Some looked like Vampyra, dressed all in black, with pale skin and red lips. A couple of people wore more elaborate costumes: One man was in a werewolf suit, and two blond girls with pigtails were wearing one dress and pretending to be Siamese twins. A headless man walked past them, carrying his head under his arm like a basketball. When they looked closer, they figured out he was wearing a special suit that hid his head in the collar of his shirt. His eyes peeked out from behind his necktie.

"That costume is awesome," Alex said admiringly.

Before the headless man could answer, two security guards rushed up to him.

"Excuse me, sir. Can I see your nametag?"

The headless man began patting his pockets, looking for his nametag. The guards grabbed him by the arms and were about to throw him out of the convention when he pulled the nametag out of his vest pocket. The guards let him go, but first they gave him a lecture.

"Whoa. They're really serious about these nametags. Or is that part of the show?" Alex said.

"I can't tell. But check out all the booths!" Tina said.

The huge hall was lined with rows of booths selling everything a horror-book fan could want. At one booth people could buy rare, first-edition copies of Emory Rex's novels. Some of them were autographed. Another booth had videos of all the movies that had been made out of Rex's books.

As Alex and Tina walked down the aisles, they saw more and more bizarre things for sale. One booth had racks of costumes. People could dress up like their favorite characters from different horror novels and have their pictures taken.

Another booth was selling props. Stretched out on the table was a fake tarantula. It had a tag that announced KEEP THE SPIDER OF GOTHRAR WITH YOU—ALWAYS! Tina walked up to the tarantula and peered at it.

"Ugh, look at all the hairs," she said.

"What about that?" Alex asked, pointing to a bloody rubber hand.

"Duh!" Tina thumped Alex on the shoulder. "Don't you remember that book, *It Came Knocking*? The bad guys cut off a guy's hand—and then the hand comes back to get revenge on them."

"Oh, yeah," Alex put his own hand on his neck. "That guy was pretty *handy*."

"Yeah—he wasn't all thumbs!" Tina said. "Hey, look at this!"

On a little velvet pillow sat a red jelly-covered object with a long rubber tube running from it. The tube ended in a little bubble. Tina picked it up and squeezed it a few times—and the red thing throbbed in response.

"Yuck! What is that?" she asked.

"I'll give you a hint," said the man who ran the booth, wagging a finger in their direction. He was a small, old man, and his nametag said JEROME HELL-ERSTEIN. "It's not from an Emory Rex novel."

"Is it from a movie?" Alex asked, but the man shook his head.

"It's from another book, right?" Tina guessed.

"An *old* book," the man said.

Tina and Alex stared at the thing. "Oh!" Tina said. "It's a heart! Right? So it must be from *My Body, My Enemy*!"

"Ach!" The man grimaced. "Kids today! I told you, it has nothing to do with Emory Rex. It's a Telltale Heart!"

Alex and Tina stared at him blankly.

"From the Edgar Allan Poe story? 'The Telltale Heart'?" He made the heart pump a few times, as if that would help them understand.

"Edgar Allan Poe? That sounds sort of familiar . . . ," Alex said.

"Listen, if you guys think Rex is scary, you should get your hands on some Poe," Jerome Hellerstein said crankily. "Now get out of here, I got hearts to sell."

Yikes! Alex felt like a dummy. "I guess there's a lot more horror we can read," he said to Tina.

"I can't wait to get to the library," she said. "Whoever this Poe guy is, he must be terrifying!"

"Get your eyeballs here, get your ice-cold eyeballs . . . ," a voice called out. Alex stopped in his tracks.

"Did she say? . . ." he asked.

"Eyeballs?" Tina finished his sentence. They both turned around and saw a teenage girl in a white coat and white hat. Her nametag said SLIM HAUT. She snapped a piece of gum in her mouth as she wheeled around a cart full of food—the most disgusting food Alex and Tina had ever seen.

"Those look real," Tina said, as she surveyed Slim's cart.

"Maybe they are," Slim answered with a wink.

The eyeballs were actually made of ice cream, and came in blue, brown, and green. Each one was wrapped individually in plastic and rested on some ice cubes. There were also squiggly worm salads made of pasta, finger sandwiches with real-looking fingers sticking out of them, Jell-O brains, and some bright green slush labeled ALIEN BLOOD.

"Yuck. I'm not hungry," Tina said.

"Three bucks for a little ice-cream eyeball? No thanks," Alex added.

"Suit yourself," the teenager said, shrugging.

"Daddy! I want an ice-cream eyeball."

"Me too! Get me one, Daddy!"

A tired-looking man with two small kids was already peeling money out of his wallet as Alex and Tina walked away from the cart. It seemed as if Slim Haut was doing a booming business selling her repulsive wares. Alex shook his head.

"People will buy *anything*," he said.

"Alex, look!" Tina grabbed his arm. "Over there."

Alex peered around, but he couldn't figure out what Tina was talking about. "What?"

"That booth. The one that says 'Emory Rex Fan Club.' Isn't that the lady from the train?"

The booth Tina was talking about had a sign above it in the same melted lettering as their name-tags. The red-haired woman with the creepy singing voice was sitting proudly at a table covered with sign-up sheets and buttons.

"Well, hey, you two." She waved energetically at Alex and Tina just as they were about to turn and walk away. "I thought you might be heading for the convention. Small world, huh?"

"We could tell you were coming here," Tina said. Alex had no idea what to say to this woman. But

Tina started chatting with her as if they were best friends.

"That's a really cool shirt," Tina said. "It's totally realistic."

"Oh, you can get one over there at my friend's booth," the woman said, pulling the shirt down so that she could admire it herself. "Ten percent discount if you're in the fan club."

"What is this fan club?" Alex finally asked.

"Just what it looks like. For serious fans only, and I'm the president." She proudly showed off her nametag: SYLVIA OWEN, EMORY REX FAN CLUB PRESIDENT. "If you join, you get a newsletter, a button, and a membership card. And like I said, if you show that card at some of the other booths, you'll get a discount on a lot of the stuff."

"Would we get to meet Emory Rex?" Tina asked excitedly. "I mean, if we were members for a long time, or if we read all his books or something?"

The smile on Sylvia Owen's face faded. "Well, probably not," she said, sounding sad.

"Have you ever met him?" Alex asked. Sylvia's eyes darkened, and she looked even more unhappy.

"He is a very mysterious, reclusive man." She sighed. "He never does public appearances at all. In fact, nobody really knows what he looks like, except his publisher."

"But you're president of the fan club!" Alex said.

Sylvia stared off into the distance, and when she spoke it was almost as if she were talking to herself. "I know. I've tried so hard to get close to him. So I could tell him how . . . *special* he is to me. But he won't respond. He won't talk to me, no matter what I do."

Sylvia looked angry now. A thin film of sweat broke out on her forehead, even in the air-conditioned convention hall. She seemed to have forgotten that Alex and Tina were standing there.

"Well . . . ," Tina said. "Maybe he's just really busy writing his books. Maybe he feels like that's the best way to thank you for being his fan." Alex stared at Tina, seriously impressed. Where had she come up with that great explanation? Tina just shrugged.

It seemed to have worked. Sylvia brightened immediately. "Why, that's a lovely way of looking at it," she said. "Listen, why don't you kids sign up for the fan club? It's only ten dollars per year for students."

Ten bucks! "Oh . . . we can't right now," Alex said.

"Maybe later. We really want to see everything first," Tina explained.

"Suit yourselves," Sylvia chirped. A couple of people approached the table, and she showed them a copy of the newsletter. "This is a very special issue," she explained as Alex and Tina slipped away. "I interviewed Emory Rex's third cousin and got the family recipe for crispy fried pan-bread. And in the next newsletter . . ."

"Wow, she *really* loves Emory Rex," Tina said, shaking her head.

"Wrong. *We* love Emory Rex. She's *obsessed* with

him!" Alex pointed out. "How come you could talk to her so easily?" he asked. "She made me feel too creeped out."

Tina shrugged. "I don't know. She seemed kind of sad and lonely. I just tried not to look at her eyes too much."

Suddenly a shout rang through the air, and people started yelling. Alex and Tina whipped around, trying to see what the commotion was. At that instant a man in a trench coat and a brown fishing hat pulled over his face pushed past them, almost knocking them over.

Tina tumbled into a booth and let out a shriek as the Tarantula of Gothrar landed on her shoulder. Alex landed facefirst in a pile of T-shirts. He flipped over and tried to get across the aisle to Tina, but people were pushing past him, running and yelling, and he could barely stand up.

He grabbed on to the tall sign on a booth and tried to look around for Tina without getting trampled. He could see Sylvia's head above the crowd. She was probably standing on top of her chair—either that, or she'd just grown about three feet. She was pointing at something and yelling, but Alex couldn't understand what she was talking about.

"It's him!" she screeched. "I saw it. I saw his nametag. It's really him!"

Things seemed to be slipping out of control. More and more people jammed into the aisle, pushing and shouting. The crowd in the convention center was turning into a mob!

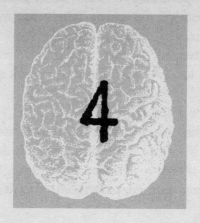

4

"A lex? *Alex!*"

He twisted around, looking for Tina. He could hear her voice, but in the crush of people he couldn't see her face.

"Back here. Turn around."

He followed the sound of her voice and saw her jammed into a doorway in a little alcove along the wall. He ducked down and pushed his way through the crowd, feeling like a linebacker for the Jets. Finally he got to the alcove and squeezed in next to Tina.

"What's going on?" Alex shouted above the noise of the crowd.

"I think I heard someone say they saw Emory Rex," she shouted back. "You know that guy who pushed us out of his way? The one in the trench coat? I think that's who they're talking about."

"Do you think it was really him?" Alex asked. "Did we really get pushed by Emory Rex?"

"I don't know." Tina grinned. "I guess maybe we had a brush with fame."

Tina and Alex waited a few minutes until the crowd calmed down. People were still moving around, but not all in the same direction. Nobody knew where the mysterious man was anymore.

"Back to normal," Alex said, stepping out of the doorway.

"Whatever normal is, in this place," Tina answered. "I guess we're not the only ones who'd like to meet Emory Rex." She leaned back against the door and felt it suddenly open behind her. *Hey!*

"Tina?" Alex stepped into the room after her. "Whoa. Look where we are!"

It was an auditorium, lined with chairs that faced a wide, curtained stage. A few stagehands were milling around, but other than that, it was silent and empty.

"What a relief," Tina sighed. "Let's just stay here."

"Can't do that," one of the stagehands said. "This room's not open to the public yet."

"What's going to happen in here?" Alex asked.

"Emory Rex reading," the stagehand said. Tina and Alex glanced at each other, both bursting with excitement. "But you're going to have to leave."

"Aw, give the kids a break," another stagehand called down from the rafters, where he was fixing lights. "Let 'em get good seats. Nobody else saw them."

"Attention, all creatures of the night!" a voice announced from a loudspeaker. "Now that you've had your stampede, we thought you'd like to know that in fifteen minutes, Emory Rex will be reading the end of *Murdernet* in the main hall. But don't panic! There's room for all of you."

The first stagehand grinned at them. "Well, it looks like this room is open to the public after all." He waved his hand, indicating the rows of empty seats. "Go ahead, pick your spots."

"All right!" Alex said. People were filing into the back of the auditorium and rushing toward the front. But Alex and Tina were ahead of the game, and they were determined to get two front-row seats.

"Whoops, not there," Tina said, pointing to one seat that had a sign taped to it. "It's reserved for Sylvia Owen."

"She might not get to meet Rex, but she sure gets VIP treatment," Alex said as he slipped into a seat nearby.

People took seats around them. Others sat on the floor and lined the back of the auditorium. Soon the place was packed. Finally Sylvia Owen came strolling in.

"The publisher saved this seat for me," she said to Alex and Tina as she sat down. "At least *someone* appreciates the work I do!"

The lights went down, and a hush fell over the hall. A spotlight shined on the scarlet curtains of the stage, and an elegant woman in a charcoal-colored suit stepped out from behind the curtains. She walked proudly to the podium on the right side of the stage and moved the microphone down a little so that she could speak into it.

"My name is Myra Manning," she announced in a steady, confident voice. "For the past fifteen years, I have had the honor of being Emory Rex's editor and the head of his publishing company, Century Books."

"Blah, blah, blah," Alex muttered.

"Rex is the shining star of Century Books," Manning went on. "In an age when blockbuster authors usually desert their smaller publishers for the big corporations, Rex has chosen to stay with us. And for that, we are eternally grateful. I have worked with Rex since the early days, and it has been a marvelous experience."

"*Mah*-velous," Tina sighed. "Why won't she bring Rex out, already?"

"As many of you die-hard fans know, today is a very special occasion. Emory Rex does not like to be seen in public. He does not do book signings. He does not go on publicity tours. He does not do appearances. But today, he's going to grace this very stage to read the conclusion of his new novel, *Murdernet*."

"If *you* ever get off the stage," Alex grumbled.

"I know you're all eager to see him. So now, without further ado, I present to you . . . Emory Rex!"

She gave a flourish with her arm and tugged on a

long, golden braided rope. The curtains swished open, revealing a wooden chair, a microphone, and a little table with a pitcher of water and a glass.

Then there was a gasp from Myra Manning—and the entire audience.

There was nobody on the stage.

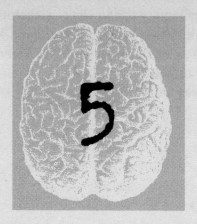

"Where is he?" Tina asked, peering up at the stage.

"I don't know. It must be some kind of trick he's playing," Alex said. He was looking up at the rafters, to see if Rex was being lowered from above. "Like that plastic dead body out front—to freak everybody out."

"Maybe he's sitting out here and he's going to walk to the stage," Tina said, twisting around and looking behind them.

People in the audience began to mutter. If this was a trick, it was lasting too long. No one seemed to think it was funny.

On stage, Myra Manning looked baffled. First she walked over to the empty chair and checked out the backstage area. She picked up a piece of paper that was lying on the chair. She read it quickly, frowned, and tucked it into a pocket in her suit. She spoke to someone offstage. *I don't know,* Tina thought she saw her saying. *Where is he?*

Then she left the stage for a few moments. Tina could see people running around backstage. The stagehands weren't smiling—they all looked puzzled.

"Wherever he is, he's not showing up yet," Tina reported, still looking around the room.

"I think something's really wrong," Alex said. "I don't think this is any kind of trick." The room was buzzing as people began talking more and more loudly. Sylvia was getting agitated, fidgeting and craning her neck to see all around the auditorium. Finally she stood up and shouted at the stage.

"What's going on?" she demanded. "Where is Emory?"

Myra Manning stepped onto the stage again. She looked pale and serious. She straightened her jacket and cleared her throat. The audience fell silent.

"Ladies and gentlemen, I am terribly sorry," Myra said in a barely controlled voice. "Mr. Rex was scheduled to be here, reading the final chapter of his book. In fact, he was here just minutes ago, and he seemed excited about this engagement. However . . ."

"Oh, no," Alex moaned. "Don't tell me."

"I am sorry to inform you all that Emory Rex . . . is not feeling well. He will not be appearing today." She tried to smile as the people in the audience began grumbling. "But please continue to enjoy the convention. All the booths are still open. Thank you."

She walked stiffly off the stage. People began shuffling out of the room, complaining loudly. Alex and Tina just sat in their seats. They were stunned.

"She wants us to enjoy the convention?" Tina asked.

Alex shook his head. "Emory Rex *is* the convention."

They sat in silence until most of the people were gone. Sylvia stayed in her seat with her face in her hands. When the crowd had thinned out, Alex and Tina made their way to the exit.

The mood of the crowd had changed completely. When they'd thought Emory Rex was going to appear before them, everyone at the convention had buzzed with excitement. Now the crowd was morose and bad-tempered.

"I don't understand how this could happen," Tina grumbled as she and Alex left the auditorium.

"There's nothing to understand," Alex snapped. "It's perfectly simple. Emory Rex isn't here. He didn't feel like showing up. Got it?"

Tina blinked a few times, then looked away without saying a word.

"I'm sorry," Alex said, feeling bad. "It's not your fault. I know you're disappointed too."

Tina nodded. There was a big lump in her throat, and she didn't want to try to talk. If she started to cry, she'd feel humiliated.

"Ah, who cares," Alex said. "Right? I mean . . ." He struggled to think of something to say. If he were Tina, he'd find the bright side of this situation and make them both feel better. "It's not as if . . ." It was no good. He couldn't think of anything cheerful.

"Well, it's not like something *happened* to him," Tina said decisively. "We'll still be able to read his books!"

"See? I *knew* there was an upside to this," Alex said.

"Yeah. I didn't want to know the end of the story anyway," Tina went on. "It's more exciting if we have to wait for the book to come out. That way we'll get to reread the whole thing—and then find out the ending."

"Hey, yeah!" Alex was feeling better already. "Come on, let's walk around again. I think I saw someone selling video games based on the books."

Tina stopped and studied a floor plan of the convention center, looking for the booth Alex wanted to visit. She noticed that the main auditorium was labeled EMORY REX, which made Tina's heart sink a little.

Tina was reading down the list of booths when the letters on the sign began to glow and move around. "Ghostwriter!" she said.

"What? Where?" Alex asked, peering at the sign. "Hey! What's he doing here?"

"Remember? He read about the convention in the paper," Tina answered. "He must have been curious about the end of the story too!"

The letters began rearranging themselves. Tina glanced around her, but nobody else noticed. That was the amazing thing about Ghostwriter. Letters would be flying around in the air, and signs would get completely scrambled while he made new words—but only the kids on the Ghostwriter Team could see it happening. To the rest of the world, the signs looked normal.

No story! Ghostwriter's message said.

"He wanted to know the ending as much as we did," Tina said sympathetically.

The letters rearranged themselves again. Where is Emory Rex? Ghostwriter's glow flashed a few times on Rex's name.

"Come on, let's sit down somewhere and write to tell him what happened," Alex suggested.

He and Tina found two metal chairs along a wall and took out one of the Emory Rex books so that Ghostwriter would have plenty of letters to work with. They opened the other book to the end, where there were a few blank pages to write on.

Emory Rex didn't show up, Tina wrote with her Ghostwriter pen, which she kept on a string around her neck. *He's not going to read the end of the story today.*

Bummer, Ghostwriter responded.

"Hey, wait a minute," Alex said, and wrote under Tina's message: *Ghostwriter, could you find the end of the story and read it to us?*

How can I find it? Ghostwriter wrote back.

That was a tough one.

"What about that piece of paper that Myra Manning took from the chair?" Tina suggested. "Maybe that was part of it. Ghostwriter could look for her nametag, and the story might be right near it."

"Awesome idea!" Alex agreed. He wrote the plan out for Ghostwriter.

Almost immediately the green glow swept over Alex's words, then disappeared. Tina jiggled her legs impatiently. Ghostwriter was out there somewhere, looking for the end of *Murdernet*—but it seemed to be taking years.

"Come on, Ghostwriter," she begged under her breath. "I've got to know what happens to Moseby!"

"Bingo!" Alex said as the green glow returned. The letters began leaping off the page and into the air in front of them:

> Emory Rex has left Silicon Valley.
> . . . He's gone to play with the dol-
> phins.

"Um . . . excuse me, Ghostwriter?" Tina said.

"What does *that* mean?" Alex asked.

Tina copied down the paragraph, then scribbled a note to Ghostwriter: *What does that mean?*

I found it near Myra Manning's name-tag, Ghostwriter said.   I don't know what it means—but Myra Manning seemed upset.

"I'll bet she is," Alex said. "Emory Rex promised to be here, and now he's backed out."

"And this must be the note he left on the chair," Tina added. "The one she put in her pocket. That's why Ghostwriter found it so easily—it was right next to her nametag."

"It sounds like he just decided to go on vacation," Alex grumbled.

"Sort of," Tina mused. "What's Silicon Valley?"

"Beats me," Alex said. "I wonder how come he said he was going to be at this convention when he really just wanted to go to some beach and play with dolphins."

"I think it might be more serious than that," Tina said, frowning at the words on the page. "I wonder if something really bad happened to Emory Rex."

"Something bad?" Alex asked. "Like what? An accident?"

"I don't know. Maybe," Tina said. "I just have a bad feeling about this. Something could be seriously wrong."

Alex patted Tina on the shoulder. "It's possible. Then again, you might just have been reading too many horror stories."

Tina smiled. "You're probably right," she said. "But it can't hurt to ask, right?"

GW, I'm wondering if something bad happened, she wrote. *Can you find any evidence that something is wrong? An ambulance? A message about an accident?*

After a few seconds, Ghostwriter answered, Nothing. But I agree. This seems very strange to me, too.

Alex and Tina leaned against the wall. They were both thinking the same thing: Was it possible that something really did happen to the famous author?

Tina felt a little chilly. She looked over at Alex and saw that he had goose bumps all over his arms.

"Maybe we're on the wrong track," Alex said. "I mean, Myra Manning might just be upset because her star author didn't show up."

"Or maybe they had some kind of argument," Tina said. "I mean, she gave that speech about how great it was that he stuck with Century Books. Maybe he decided to go with another publisher, and that's why he didn't show up."

"Hey, yeah!" Alex's eyes were bright. "Or maybe she thought—"

"What? Maybe she thought what?" Tina yanked on his sleeve. She didn't like the look on his face.

"What if that lady from Century Books really wanted *Murdernet* to sell well? What do you think she'd do?"

"I don't know," Tina said. "I guess she'd have her star author read the end of his book at a convention. Just like they planned."

"Yeah . . . but what if he didn't show up? What if he just vanished? People would already have bought their tickets. They'd go crazy! There would be all sorts of publicity. It would be on the evening news and everything." Alex thumped his fist into his hand. "I'll just bet they planned it this way!"

"You mean they *purposely* said Emory Rex would show up, even though they knew he wouldn't?" Tina scowled. "But that's lying. It's false advertising. They wouldn't do that, would they?"

"I don't know," Alex admitted. "Myra Manning

looked pretty upset. But she might have been acting. There's only one way to tell for sure. We have to go to the offices of Century Books and look around."

A lex and Tina looked up Century Books in the phone directory. It wasn't far from the hotel, but they had to take the subway to get there. This time they took the N train to Fifty-ninth Street, then got off and walked a few blocks south.

The neighborhood was completely different from where Tina and Alex lived, in Brooklyn. It was only about a mile away, across the East River—but it might as well have been in Paris. Lexington Avenue was lined with tiny shops that were crammed with expensive clothes, jewelry, shoes, and antiques.

The sidewalk was jammed with people. Just walking one block was like busting through the Giants offensive line. And everyone seemed to be in a hurry—especially the messengers, mostly young guys with bicycles and huge bags slung over their shoulders.

Tina felt very grown-up and a little nervous. She was walking around Manhattan with Alex! Her parents were nowhere near. It was the kind of thing she always wished she could do. Still, she kept wishing her parents knew where she was.

"Here it is," Alex announced suddenly, stopping short on the sidewalk. Tina bumped into him, then looked up.

The building towered above them, all concrete and glass. It looked old-fashioned, with tall windows that were rounded at the top and gold paint decorating the area above the doors and around each window. Across the front, over the bank of six revolving doors, CENTURY BOOKS was etched into the concrete.

Alex went through the revolving doors. Tina hopped in after him. But instead of coming out on the lobby side, Alex went all the way around in a circle until he was back out on the sidewalk again.

"Hey!" Tina yelled. But Alex pushed the door too fast for her to stop it, and before she knew it she was standing on the sidewalk too.

"I'm dizzy," she complained, putting her hands on her hips. "What's going on?"

"Take a look," Alex answered, pointing inside the glass doors.

Tina saw at least ten security guards, stopping everybody who tried to get into the building. The hallway was full of people, all shouting at the security guards. Some of them were holding notebooks, tape recorders, and cameras.

The revolving doors whipped around again, and two men stormed out.

"I can't believe this," the first one complained angrily. "This press pass usually gives me access everywhere. The place is locked tighter than a drum."

"They aren't saying a word about the Rex disappearance," the other man answered. "We've got to get a quote from somebody for the late edition."

The men hurried off. Alex watched them, stroking his chin thoughtfully.

"Whatever's going on, it's happening in there," he said. "We have to get past those security guards and into the Century offices if we're going to find out anything."

"Maybe we should tell them we're on assignment from the school paper," Tina suggested.

"Are you kidding me? That guy's press pass said he was from *The Daily Post*! If they didn't let him in, they aren't going to let two kids from Hurston Middle School in." Alex shook his head. "There's only one way for us to get in there. We've got to sneak past while all those grown-ups are fighting it out."

"*Sneak* past? I don't know," Tina said doubtfully. "Maybe we should just wait until the newspaper stories come out."

"Come on, Tina," Alex said. "When Emory Rex didn't show up, it was the most disappointing thing ever. But if he's disappeared, we have a chance to find him! We've got to follow up on this."

"But what if we get caught?" Tina peered through the glass doors at the guards.

"We won't get caught," Alex promised. "Those guys wouldn't notice if a whole pack of wild dogs ran past their feet. They've got too much on their minds."

"Let's just watch for a minute," Tina said. "Maybe we'll see another way to get in."

Alex let out a long, frustrated sigh. He leaned against the side of the building and gazed at the guards inside.

Tina pressed her forehead against the glass and watched too.

"Check it out," she said, pointing at one of the messengers. He showed his bag to the guards. They asked him for identification, and he pulled out his wallet. Then they waved him through.

Alex turned to Tina. He was grinning, and his eyes narrowed mischieviously.

"Are you thinking what I'm thinking?" he asked.

"That depends. Are you thinking that we could sneak in with a messenger?" Tina responded, tilting her head thoughtfully.

"You got it!" Alex said. "All we have to do is wait for the next messenger. We'll stick close by him, and they'll think we're with him. And he'll be in such a hurry to get away from the reporters, he'll never even notice us."

Alex and Tina lingered around the crowded entrance, trying to look inconspicuous. Before they knew it, a large, burly man with long dreadlocks came striding up to the door. He was dressed entirely in black spandex and had a bicycle slung over one shoulder. On the other was a bright orange messenger pack. He swung open one of the nonrevolving doors. Alex and Tina slipped in after him. He strode up to the head security guard.

"I don't care who you work for," the guard was

telling an angry young man with short hair and a goatee. "And I don't care what your editor says. You're not getting into this building—"

" 'Scuse me, I got a delivery," the bike messenger interrupted.

"Oh, hey, Jimmy," the guard said. "Go ahead. Going up to the tenth floor?"

"Just like always," the bike messenger said. He patted the bag on his shoulder. "They told me this was a superultimate rush delivery."

That seemed to really get the reporters excited. "Tenth floor?" the man with the goatee shouted, his eyes practically popping out of his head. "What's on the tenth floor?" He shoved a tape recorder into Jimmy's face. "Is this package going to Myra Manning's office?"

"Hey, man! Be cool," Jimmy said. "I can't tell you that. I'm a messenger. I'm supposed to keep my clients' business secret."

With that he turned his back on the crowd of reporters and walked toward the elevators. Alex and Tina stayed close behind him and slipped past the guards.

Tina felt a little line of sweat trickling down her hairline. *Stop being so nervous,* she scolded herself. *So what if we get caught? The worst thing they can do is throw us out of the building.* But her heart was in her throat as she followed Jimmy toward the elevators.

"It looks like we're home free," Alex whispered. He peeked behind him. "I think we made it!"

Tina couldn't help herself. She just had to look

back. She peeked over her shoulder to see if anyone was following them.

She was expecting to see the backs of all the guards. Instead she looked straight into the eyes of the head of security for the Century Books building.

He paused. Then he squinted.

Then he pointed right at Tina and Alex.

Tina felt her heart plummet straight into her shoes as he started to yell.

"Hey, you kids. Get back here. Where do you think you're going?"

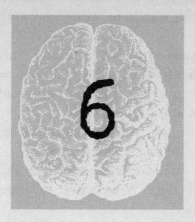

6

Jimmy turned around, glanced at Alex and Tina, and waved his free hand at the head security guard.

"It's all right," he called back. "They're with me."

Alex was already turning around to walk out of the building, but he spun back and fell into step beside Jimmy. Tina gaped at Jimmy in disbelief, then looked at the guard again.

He didn't look convinced. "They're with you?" he asked incredulously.

"Yep. Foot messengers. In training," Jimmy explained.

The reporter with the goatee noticed that the head security guard was distracted and tried to sneak around the other side of the desk. Two of the guards grabbed him, and there was a big commotion.

"All right, all right!" the head guard yelled, waving

his hand at Jimmy, Tina, and Alex. He had too much on his hands to worry about a couple of kids.

Jimmy stepped onto the elevator with Alex and Tina practically glued to his sides. Alex was smiling so hard, he looked as if his face were ready to crack open. Tina was just bewildered.

"I'm with him too!" they heard the reporter yell as the doors of the elevators closed.

"Phew!" Jimmy leaned against the wall of the elevator. "All right. Now, where *do* you two think you're going?"

"We're trying to figure out what happened to Emory Rex," Alex said. "He disappeared today, and we thought it might be a publicity stunt."

"So we wanted to investigate," Tina continued. "This seemed like the best place to start."

"Pint-sized supersleuths, huh?" Jimmy nodded. "I thought it was something like that. That's why I let you come in with me. I was a nosy little kid too. Plus, I had the same idea about coming to Century Books myself."

"What do you mean?" Alex asked. "You're a bike messenger, aren't you?"

"Well, that's how I make money while I'm in school." He pulled out his wallet and showed them an identification card from New York University: NYU JOURNALISM—JIMMY CLAY. "I'm studying to be a reporter. I heard about Rex's disappearance while I was on my messenger rounds, and I thought I'd use my job to get into the Century Books offices.

If I can get this story before anyone else, it'll help me get a job when I graduate."

"So what's in your messenger bag?" Tina asked.

Jimmy patted the orange sack fondly. "Just my lunch," he said.

"Wow. That's so *sneaky*," Tina said admiringly.

"Tina's a reporter too," Alex pointed out. "She does video news reports for Hurston Middle School."

"Hey," Jimmy said, giving Tina a wide smile. She smiled back proudly, even though her face was red as a beet. "Well, maybe we'll be working together someday, Tina."

"Um . . . yeah, maybe," she said. "I mean, I hope so."

The elevator finally arrived at the tenth floor.

"Well, you guys stay out of trouble," Jimmy cautioned. "I'm going to see if I overhear anything in the back offices. You kids can probably sneak around to the front office—it's that way—and listen to what's going on. It's so busy, nobody will even notice you."

"Thanks a lot for getting us in," Alex said.

"You can pay me back by telling me anything you find out," Jimmy said with a smile. "See you guys out there, huh?"

"Yeah. See you later, Jimmy," Alex said.

"Bye," Tina added. Jimmy waved and walked down a dingy, cluttered corridor. Alex and Tina went the opposite way, where Jimmy had pointed, toward the front of the building.

"This place sure is messy," Tina said. In each office they passed, desks were piled high with thick files. Boxes of papers were stacked in the halls. A half-empty water cooler was slowly leaking water onto the gray carpet.

The hallway led into a large room divided into cubicles, with a desk and a computer in each. But the desks were mostly empty. Most of the workers were rushing around or talking frantically on the phone. A lot of them stood in groups, arguing about what should be done next. It was a madhouse. Through it all, the phones kept ringing with loud electronic bleats.

"It sure is busy in here," Alex said. He nudged Tina. "Hey, look! That doorway says 'Myra Manning'."

At the far end of the large room was a glass-walled corner office. Quietly Alex and Tina made their way across the crowded room and stood behind a file cabinet near the office. A frazzled-looking woman with her head in her hands sat at a desk just outside the office. She didn't even look up, and nobody else seemed to notice Alex and Tina either.

Suddenly the phone rang. The assistant grabbed the receiver. "Myra Manning's office," she said into the phone. "Barbara Casey speaking. No, I don't have any information on Emory Rex. I'm sorry. I have no comment." She sounded as if she was close to tears.

"Barbara!" a voice roared out of the office. "Have you located Rex's summer home?"

Barbara Casey looked up at the ceiling. "Oh, boy," she moaned.

"*Barbara!*" Myra Manning burst out of her office and stood in front of her assistant's desk. She was still wearing her charcoal-colored suit from the convention—but the rest of her looked very different. Her hair was uncombed, she wasn't wearing shoes, and her face was flushed. She had an angry scowl on her face. "Do you have information for me or not?"

"I have some information. But you're not going to like it," Barbara said in a trembling voice. Everyone in the office stopped moving. They were like animals in the forest who hear a hunter coming. They peered through frightened eyes at Myra, who was glaring at her assistant.

"If you have information," she said, tapping her foot on the floor, "I would like to hear what it is."

Barbara Casey took a deep breath. She brushed her curly blond hair off her face and opened her notebook.

"Emory Rex's home number isn't his home at all. That's why we always get his answering machine. It's just a voice-mail center where he picks up messages. Same thing with his summer house number, except that's connected to an answering service in the Caribbean."

"So you're saying there is no way to track down where he might be," Myra Manning said in a quiet, angry voice.

"Um, no." Barbara grimaced. "I mean, yes. That's what I'm saying."

"Great. Great!" Myra shook her fists at the ceiling. "That's just great!" Then she used a couple of words that Alex had heard his father use only once, when the refrigeration system at their bodega broke down. "My number one author completely disappears from a convention, right before he's about to do the most important appearance of his career. And nobody here can find him!" She looked around the room at the terrified faces.

"Well, don't just stand there!" she shouted at everyone. "Find Emory Rex!" She stormed back into her office and slammed the door behind her. Barbara Casey burst into tears, and everybody began scurrying around again. The fax machine next to Barbara began humming, and her phone rang again. She put her head down on the desk and covered her ears with her hands.

"Wow," Alex whispered to Tina. "I guess Rex really disappeared. This definitely isn't faked."

"Look! There's Ghostwriter," Tina whispered back.

The green glow was buzzing back and forth across the shiny fax paper as it came out of the machine. Then Ghostwriter whizzed over to Alex and Tina, bringing them the message from the fax.

There was no return phone number across the top of the fax. There were only a few sentences:

It was a tiny island across the bay from Jamaica. The dolphins swam there, even in winter, and rabbits frolicked in the grass.

It seemed like paradise, the place where Rex had found his Queen.

Only this paradise didn't last forever. In fact, this paradise was about to become the last place he wanted to be.

And there wasn't much chance that he'd leave this place alive.

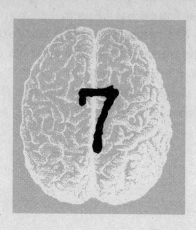

7

Watching the letters hanging in the air above him, Alex felt confused—and scared.

"What does it mean?" he murmured. He didn't know the answer to his question. But he was sure it wasn't good news.

Tina finished copying the message into the back pages of her Emory Rex book, under the earlier Ghostwriter message. She looked up at Alex with a small smile.

"You know, at first this mystery was just really scary to me," she said. "But now it's getting exciting!"

Good old Tina, Alex thought. Just when he was beginning to lose hope, she was getting totally into the case. Alex could feel himself getting more curious about it too.

Just then Barbara Casey spotted the fax. She

leaped up from her desk and ripped the fax out of the machine. "Ms. Manning!" she called out as she ran into the office. "This fax. I think it's important!"

The other workers quickly gathered around Myra Manning's office, peering in as she and Barbara read the fax. One or two of them glanced at Tina and Alex as if noticing them for the first time.

"I think we've found out everything we can," Alex muttered. "Maybe we should get out of here." He looked around. "Now."

"Wait. Don't you want to see what Myra has to say about the fax?" Tina said.

"Tina, people are starting to notice us. We've got to get out of here." Alex tugged on her arm.

"Okay, okay," Tina groaned, looking longingly at Myra's office.

They ducked out of the room and ran for the elevator. Jimmy was already there. He held the door open for them and hit the button for the lobby.

"So? What did you find out?" Jimmy asked as soon as the doors closed.

"Well, this definitely wasn't a publicity stunt," Tina said. "Emory Rex has disappeared. And nobody knows where he is."

"He left phone numbers that nobody can trace," Alex added. "And somebody sent this weird fax." He showed the words to Jimmy, who shook his head and let out a long, low whistle.

"Looks like trouble," Jimmy said. "But it's pretty confusing, too. Do you guys have any idea what it means?"

"Nope." Tina shook her head.

"What did you find?" Alex asked.

"Well, I don't know if this is important or not," Jimmy said. "But I looked through some old files when nobody was around. I went back about twenty years, and I found out that Emory Rex used to have a partner."

"A partner?" Tina asked. "You mean someone he would write his stories with?"

"Right. Some guy named Frank Bowman. But halfway through the first book, Bowman dropped out of sight. His name was on the original contract, but when the book came out—*poof!* He had disappeared. His name wasn't even on the book."

"Weird," Alex said.

"It gets better. There are also some legal papers back there. Bowman got pretty upset about being dropped by Rex and by Century Books. He sued, and there was a settlement. Century had to give him some money. But he still never got published by them. And his name never went on that first book—even when they reprinted it."

"Wow! This is getting really good!" Tina's eyes were shining. "I know all this stuff goes together somehow. But how? Where did Rex go? And why did Frank Bowman get dropped from that first book?"

The elevator doors opened at the lobby.

"Good luck, you guys," Jimmy said. "I'm going to go see if the *Post* will run my story about Rex's disappearance. I'll be miles ahead of those reporters."

He was gone in a flash, rushing out the front doors and speeding away on his bicycle.

"I told you guys, nobody's coming in here." The head security man was still arguing with the reporter with the goatee.

"Hey, check it out," Alex said, pointing to the main entrance. Several police officers and two guys in dark suits and sunglasses were just coming in through the revolving doors.

"We're going to have to ask you people to leave," one of the police officers said to the reporters as he entered the lobby. "I'm sorry, but you're blocking a public area."

"Hey, come on," one of the security guards objected. "We've got this thing under—" He stopped short as one of the dark-suited men flashed an ID at him. Alex heard him mutter, "FBI." Alex and Tina sidled out the front doors along with the reporters.

"What did he say? Who were those guys?" Tina asked. But Alex shook his head. Tina clamped her mouth shut and kept quiet until they were out on the sidewalk. She whispered her question again.

"They were from the FBI," Alex said.

"FBI?"

"Federal Bureau of Investigation. It's a government agency that investigates really big crimes. Like bombings, or counterfeiting, or . . ." His voice trailed off and his eyes widened.

"Or what?" Tina asked, shaking him. "Alex, what?"

"That's it," he breathed. "There's only one reason the FBI would get called in on a disappearance like this. They investigate *kidnappings!*"

Tina yelped. "You're right. That's it."

Emory Rex had been kidnapped!

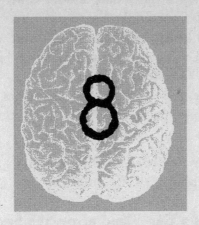

``That's right. Kidnapped!" Tina announced.
The rest of the team sat in stunned silence.

As soon as they left Century Books, Alex and Tina had hurried home and written *RALLY—A* in the back of the Emory Rex book. It was the Ghostwriter Team's secret way of calling a meeting. Ghostwriter had taken the message to everyone else on the team—at least, everyone who was around. Now Jamal, Lenni, and Hector were with Alex and Tina in Alex's room. Tina and Alex had explained the entire story, ending with the FBI showing up in the lobby of the Century offices.

"Now I wish I'd gone to that stupid convention," Lenni grumbled.

"Told ya so," Tina said with a sniff.

"We've got to start a casebook," Hector insisted.

He went over to Alex's desk and sat down. "Do you have an extra notebook, Alex?"

"Just for emergencies like this," Alex answered. He opened a drawer and pulled out a blue spiral notebook. "Go ahead, Hector."

"Let's see. First, let's put down the clues." Hector copied the two mysterious notes onto a clues page:

Emory Rex has left Silicon Valley . . . he's gone to play with the dolphins.

It was a tiny island across the bay from Jamaica. The dolphins swam there, even in winter, and rabbits frolicked in the grass. It seemed like paradise, the place where Rex had found his Queen.

Only this paradise didn't last forever. In fact, this paradise was about to become the last place he wanted to be.

And there wasn't much chance that he'd leave this place alive.

Then Hector flipped a few pages forward. "Now, the suspects. Any ideas?"

"Who would want to kidnap a writer?" Jamal said.

"Oh, I know!" Hector shot out of his chair. "I read about this movie once. It was about this lady who fell in love with the guy who wrote her favorite romance novels. She kidnapped him and tortured him. She even broke his leg."

"What's your point, Hector?" Lenni asked. "We're supposed to be thinking of suspects."

"That's my suspect. The crazy fan club lady Alex and Tina met. The one who was singing on the train. She said she was mad that Rex didn't talk to her. Maybe she kidnapped him."

"Hmmmm. Sylvia Owen. It's an idea," Tina said. "We may as well put her down."

"But she was sitting right next to us when he disappeared," Alex objected. "There's no way it could be her."

"But she might be involved," Tina pointed out. "She's pretty obsessed with Rex. She might have masterminded the kidnapping, then planted herself in the crowd so nobody would suspect her."

"Wow." Alex was impressed. "I guess I didn't think of that."

Tina wrote Sylvia Owen's name on the suspects list.

"Well, I have my own idea," Alex said. "I think it was Frank Bowman."

"Frank Bowman?" Lenni said. "But he hasn't been involved with Emory Rex for the last twenty years."

"Maybe that's the point." Alex's mind was going a million miles an hour. "Maybe he never got over the fact that Rex dumped him. He's been angry and jealous all these years. He finally decided to kidnap Rex—to get revenge."

"Wow, that really makes sense," Tina said. "I'll put that in the casebook too."

"What about that assistant lady?" Lenni suggested.

"You mean Barbara Casey?" Tina asked. "How could she have done anything?"

"I don't know. Maybe dealing with Myra Manning is driving her crazy. Maybe she wants to ruin her boss by getting rid of the biggest author at Century Books!"

"But Myra's driving her even more crazy now that Rex is gone," Alex pointed out.

"She could still be involved," Lenni said. "It sounds like her job is really stressful."

"Hmmm." Tina thought that idea was pretty unlikely. She didn't want to hurt Lenni's feelings, so she wrote it down.

The team surveyed the suspects list. One weird lady, one mystery guy, and a desperate assistant. And Emory Rex was still missing.

"Maybe we should take another look at these strange notes," Tina suggested, turning the pages back again. "Does anyone have any idea what they could mean?"

" 'This paradise was about to become the last place he wanted to be.' " Lenni wrinkled her nose. "Not to be picky, but these notes are totally melodramatic."

"It's funny—they seem sort of familiar," Alex added. "I could swear I'd heard them before."

"Silicon Valley . . . Silicon Valley . . . Now I remember. I read that recently, and I remember where it was," Tina said. "My dad told me it's a place in

California where there are a lot of computer software companies."

"Software companies, huh?" Alex shook his head. "Do you think maybe Rex was dabbling in computers, and someone got angry about it and kidnapped him?"

"Maybe," Tina said absently. "Or—*that's it!*" She sat up abruptly.

"What's it?" Hector asked.

"I remember where I read about Silicon Valley. It was in *Murdernet*! Remember, Alex?"

"Hey, yeah!" Alex grinned back at her excitedly. "What issue was that in?"

"I don't know. Come on, we'll find it," she said, picking up one of the back issues of *Gotham City Horror Chronicles*. "It was early in the story. So it was probably an early issue."

"Um, guys—" Jamal said.

"The early issues are probably under my bed," Alex said. "I'll get them. The mess under there is a *real* horror."

"Guys?" Jamal said again.

"Rats! This one picks up right after that part," Tina complained, dropping her issue on the floor. "Alex, we'll have to go to my house if you can't find that issue."

Jamal looked at Lenni and shrugged. Then he uncapped his Ghostwriter pen and wrote in the casebook:

> *GW, can you find a sentence that's just like this*

in one of the Emory Rex stories in Gotham City Horror Chronicles?

Emory Rex has left Silicon Valley . . . he's gone to play with the dolphins.

Alex sat back on his hands when the green glow breezed past him into the stack of magazines. "Oh, yeah," he said. "I forgot. Ghostwriter can find it faster than we can!"

Ghostwriter zoomed through the magazines at top speed. In a few minutes one of the magazines started throbbing with a bright green light.

"I guess that's it," Alex said, sliding that issue out of the stack and opening it. *Thanks, GW!* he scribbled in the margin.

Ghostwriter had found an early section of *Murdernet.* Moseby, the hero, was still just a lonely computer programmer with no friends. Then a mysterious stranger offered him a new job if he would relocate to a Caribbean island. When he got to his new job, Moseby was happy. But one day, when he was poking around on the Internet, he found a newspaper article about his own disappearance. It said people searching his apartment to look for him had found this note:

Eric Moseby has left Silicon Valley . . . he's gone to play with the dolphins.

"But in our note, it says *Rex* has left Silicon Valley," Lenni said. "So someone put Rex's name into Rex's story."

"Look, Ghostwriter found the other message," Jamal said. They pulled out the issue and read that one too.

It was a tiny island across the bay from Jamaica. The dolphins swam there, even in winter, and rabbits frolicked in the grass. It seemed like paradise, the place where Moseby had found his Queen.

Only this paradise didn't last forever. In fact, this paradise was about to become the last place he wanted to be.

And there wasn't much chance that he'd leave this place alive.

"They did it again," Lenni said. "They just stuck Rex's name in. What's the point?"

"Well, I don't know," Alex admitted. "But this is the part of the story when Moseby meets Janet in the Caribbean. She's the one he has to save later."

"Rabbits, dolphins, paradise—this must mean something," Jamal said. "But I have no idea what!"

Tina had a thought that gave her chills. "Maybe the kidnapper is really sick," she said. "Maybe the kidnapper is so angry at Rex that he—or she—is using Rex's own words as teasing clues. So if he doesn't get rescued, Rex gets demolished just like the characters in his own stories."

"What a way to go," Hector said with a shiver.

"That makes it even more important that we figure out what these clues mean," Alex said. "Maybe Rex is being held on a Caribbean island, just like Eric Moseby!"

"Yeah. Maybe he's been kidnapped and brought to Jamaica," Hector said. "Jamal, what do you think? Jamal? *Jamal?*"

Jamal was staring off into space.

"Helloooo! Earth to Jamal!" Hector called out. "Do you read me?"

"Nametags," Jamal murmured thoughtfully.

"Uh-oh. I think this case has sent Jamal off the deep end," Lenni said, throwing a pillow at him.

"Hey!" Jamal tossed the pillow back. "Quit it. I was just thinking about the nametags at the convention. You said that absolutely everybody was wearing them, right?"

"Absolutely everybody," Tina agreed, remembering the security guards. "Otherwise those big goons would throw you out."

"Even Myra Manning—and Emory Rex?" Jamal asked.

"Uh-huh. That's why he almost got trampled," Alex said.

"Then Ghostwriter can find him—or his nametag, at least. He can find the name of the hotel and look around it for *Emory Rex.*"

"Whoa! Jamal, major brainpower," Alex said.

Tina wrote down the plan for Ghostwriter. He whipped around her words a few times and took off.

"Wait a minute," Alex said. "Maybe that wasn't

such a hot idea. I mean, we were at the convention hours ago. Emory Rex wouldn't still be sticking around there, would he?"

"He would if he was being held hostage," Jamal said. "Maybe nobody saw him leave because he *didn't* leave. Maybe he's being held prisoner in one of the hotel rooms. Or in some smelly old basement."

"Bingo! Here comes Ghostwriter," Lenni announced. The green glow was back, and it was lighting up the words *Horror Convention: Emory Rex.*

That's awesome, GW! Tina wrote back. *Now, what—*

She stopped writing abruptly. Something very strange was happening.

Ghostwriter could make letters do a lot of things. Sometimes he made them fly around before he formed them into words. Sometimes he made them sparkle or blink. And he could make them big or small. But right now, the letters weren't doing any of those things.

They were just sort of crumpling.

As the team watched, the letters in the name *Emory Rex* started to slowly fold into themselves, becoming mangled and then disappearing, piece by piece.

What's going on? Tina wrote hurriedly.

I'm not sure, Ghostwriter responded. The letters just sort of fell apart!

Can you find anything nearby? Tina asked.

Ghostwriter whisked away again and returned quickly. **Clean Streets Carting Company,** he reported.

"I think that's a garbage truck company," Hector said. "I see them outside my building sometimes."

"A garbage truck?" Tina asked. Then she gasped and covered her mouth.

"It's no big deal," Jamal said. "Rex must have taken off the nametag. Or maybe the kidnappers took it off for him and threw it in the trash."

"And then it got crunched up by the truck," Lenni added. "That's why it disappeared like that."

But Alex had read a lot of Emory Rex. And he knew just where Tina's mind was going.

And there wasn't much chance that he'd leave this place alive.

"You'd better hope somebody took that nametag off Emory Rex," Alex said solemnly. "Because if they didn't . . . he just got pulverized."

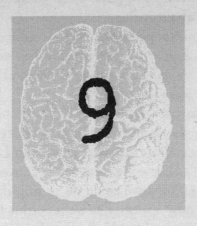

Alex and Tina stared at the empty space where the name *Emory Rex* used to be. So did the rest of the Ghostwriter Team. They were all imagining the same thing: Emory Rex, the famous author, getting crunched up by a garbage truck. They all gave a shudder.

"I can't get that picture out of my head," Hector said. "All I can think about is those letters getting mashed. Then I think of Emory Rex getting mashed."

"It's grossing me out," Jamal complained. "I wish we'd never thought about it."

"Come on, you guys. Think of something else," Tina begged. "There has to be more stuff we can figure out about this case."

Lenni stood up. "My dad's playing a gig tonight, and I promised I'd be upstairs before he left," she said. "Come on, you guys. We'll go up to my place and think about it there."

The team trooped upstairs. Tina stopped at Alex's desk to pick up the casebook and the two copies of *Gotham City Horror Chronicles*. She and Alex were the last to leave the room.

"The more we think about this case, the less sense it makes," she complained as they walked through the bodega and up the stairs that led to Lenni's loft. "I just can't believe we were at the convention, and there was nothing we could do to stop this kidnapping. And now it seems like we're getting farther and farther away from any kind of explanation."

"Don't worry," Alex said. They were standing outside Lenni's door. He patted Tina on the shoulder. He wanted to say something to make her feel better. But he couldn't think what to say.

"It's just really frustrating, you know?" Tina continued. "Here's this guy. He's totally famous, and he's surrounded by people in the middle of a fancy hotel in midtown Manhattan. Next thing you know, he just vanishes. And nobody saw who took him." She put a hand on her hip and stared into the street angrily. "Then somebody starts sending these weird cryptic messages, taken straight out of his books. And nothing makes any sense."

Alex opened his mouth to speak. But Tina was on a roll. Which was fine with him, because he still didn't know what to say.

"And to top it all off, the rest of the team wasn't even there when he disappeared. Everyone is relying on us to remember every detail of the convention. There's so much pressure on me to remember, I'm not even sure if I went to the convention anymore." She shook her head.

Alex was ready to kick himself. He was standing next to one of his closest friends—who happened to be a really pretty girl—and she was feeling really bad. He couldn't think of a single thing to tell her that would make her feel better.

Tina turned to Alex. To his surprise, she had a small, relieved smile on her face.

"Wow, Alex. Thank you so much for listening. I really had to get that off my chest!" Tina said. She gave him a friendly kiss on the cheek and walked through Lenni's door.

Alex held the door open as Tina went in. He stared after her, baffled. "Uh . . . no problem," he said.

"Thanks for listening?" he repeated to himself. "I had no idea it was that easy."

Inside Lenni's loft, the rest of the team had already turned on the television. Everyone was lying around in the living area.

"You guys, what are you doing?" Tina complained. "We're supposed to be working on a case, not sitting around watching—"

"It's a special report!" Lenni yelled, pointing at the television set. "Tina, check it out. They're talking about Emory Rex!"

". . . that apparently Emory Rex has been kidnapped," the announcer said in a grave voice.

"We were right!" Tina whispered raptly. "Alex, that's why the FBI was there!"

"Investigators have found one lead in this bizarre case," the announcer continued. "Two threatening notes were left by the kidnapper, who apparently knows Rex's books very well. These notes have led the investigators to the Caribbean. We were not able to see the notes or find out what they said. But the investigators in charge have assured us that this is the best strategy, and that they will soon find the famous author."

The report ended, and Lenni clicked the television off. "Well, I guess they're going to find him," she said.

"I don't know about that," said Tina.

"What do you mean?" Jamal asked. "The newscaster said that the FBI guys were really sure of themselves. And the notes did say something about Jamaica. The kidnapper must have taken Rex down there and then sent back those clues."

But Tina wasn't satisfied. "It doesn't feel right to me," she said. "I mean, it is just so obvious. Why would the kidnapper leave such easy clues?"

"She's got a point," Alex said. "Why would the kidnapper want to be followed? There has to be more to it than that."

"Let's take another look at that casebook," Lenni said. "All we've got is these two notes. I don't see what's so special about them."

"There's the Clean Streets Carting Company clue

too," said Jamal. "We should add that to the casebook."

"I'll do it," said Hector. "Then tell Ghostwriter what's going on." He wrote down the information about the investigators' trip to the Caribbean while the rest of the team pored over the casebook.

" 'Left Silicon Valley for the dolphins,' " Jamal read. "It sure sounds like a Caribbean island. Where else would there be dolphins? And he says in the next note that it's across the bay from Jamaica."

"But look at this other part, about rabbits frolicking in the grass." Lenni frowned. "When I think of Caribbean islands, I don't think of rabbits."

"I know," Alex said. "What's up with that? And finding his Queen . . . I love Emory Rex and all, but I've got to admit, it's kind of corny of him to call Janet his Queen."

"Jamaica. His Queen." Hector said the words aloud as he thought about it. "Jamaica. Queen. Hey . . . Jamaica, Queens! That's a neighborhood that's part of New York City! You guys, maybe he's not in the Caribbean. Maybe he's right here in New York!"

"You mean he's been here the whole time?" Alex asked, shaking his head.

"That must be where he's holding Rex," Jamal said. "Now all we have to do is see which one of our suspects lives there."

"We can call Information," Hector suggested. "We'll give them the names, and they'll tell us who's listed in the telephone directory."

"Good thinking," Tina said. "But what if the kidnapper doesn't have a phone?"

"We'll worry about that when we have to," Alex said, picking up the phone. "First let's see if we can find something."

But three calls to Information left them nowhere. There was no Frank Bowman in Queens. There was no Barbara Casey. And there was no Sylvia Owen.

"Well?" Tina asked Alex. "I guess we *do* have to worry about the kidnapper not having a phone."

"We'll have to send Ghostwriter out to search the whole borough," Hector said. "He'll go street by street, looking for any one of the names. One of them has to be there somewhere!"

"Hector, that's crazy," Lenni said. "It'll take forever. And we still might not find the kidnapper. There has to be a better way."

"Wait a minute. Let's take another look at those notes," Jamal said. He grabbed the casebook and started to read. Then he bonked himself on the head. "I thought so!"

"What? What did you think?" Hector wanted to know.

"We missed a part of the clue," Jamal pointed out. "This says the island is 'across the bay from Jamaica.' We've been looking *in* Jamaica."

"Duh!" Lenni said. She stood up and grabbed a folded-up subway map from the bookshelf. "I can't believe we missed that. But I can't remember a bay here in the city."

"There's Sheepshead Bay," Tina said. "That's where my mom gets fresh fish sometimes."

"There's Bayonne," Hector piped up. "It's a town in New Jersey where my friend's grandmother lives."

"Hey, look! There's a Bayside in Queens," Alex pointed out.

"Uh . . . thanks for all that useful information," Lenni said. "Let's just take a look at the map, okay?"

She traced her finger around the map until she found Jamaica, Queens. Right next to it was a blue body of water.

" 'Jamaica Bay,' " Lenni read. "I never even heard of it before. It's right there!"

"Now, what island could they be talking about?" Alex asked. "Across the bay from Jamaica. What about that island there? Rockaway Island?"

"There's Coney Island, but it's not really an island," Tina pointed out. That was true. Coney Island used to be an island, but now it was really more like a little bump of land that stuck out from the rest of Brooklyn. But it was still called Coney Island.

"Does it have dolphins on it?" Hector asked.

"No!" Lenni scoffed. "There's no dolphins in New Yo—" She stopped short. "Wait a minute. Yes, there are. The New York Aquarium is in Coney Island!"

"That's right!" Jamal cheered. "And there's an amusement park too."

"What about the rabbits?" Hector wanted to know.

"Maybe the rabbits are just there to throw us off,"

Jamal said hopefully. "They probably have nothing to do with the location of the kidnapper."

"Maybe there's a ride in the amusement park," Alex suggested with a grin. "A new roller coaster called the Rabbitron."

"Guys, be serious," Tina moaned. "I wish we had an encyclopedia."

"We've got a dictionary," Lenni said. "Maybe Coney Island will be in there." She leafed through the *C*s. "*Canteloupe . . . Chevrolet . . . condiment*—" She stopped suddenly. "Hmm!"

"*Hmm*, you found Coney Island?" Alex asked. "Or *hmm*, it's not in there?"

"*Hmm*, both," Lenni said. "Coney Island isn't in here. But the word *coney* is. And check out what it means!"

Tina looked over her shoulder. "That's it!" she said. "*Coney* is an old English word for rabbit. It's another clue—the kidnapper is definitely in Coney Island."

"Let's call Information again," Jamal said. "Only this time, we'll look for suspects in Coney Island."

"We don't need to call this time," Lenni pointed out. "I've got the Brooklyn phone book right here."

There was no listing for Barbara Casey. But when they looked up Frank Bowman and Sylvia Owen, they hit pay dirt.

"Wow! They're both here!" Lenni exclaimed.

"Well, which one is it?" Hector asked. "Which one lives in Coney Island?"

"I can't tell," Tina answered, copying the street

addresses into the casebook next to each person's name. "If we had their zip codes or a detailed map, we could find out."

Sylvia Owen lived at 802 President Street. Frank Bowman's address was listed simply as Bowery and West Fifteenth Street. There was no way to tell which one of them was in a Coney Island neighborhood.

"Hey, I know how we could figure it out," Lenni piped up. "There's this really, really detailed map of Brooklyn that I saw one time. It had absolutely every street on it. I looked ours up. And on each block, it also has the house numbers."

"Good going, Lenni," Alex said. "Where is it?"

Lenni's face fell. "At the library," she said.

Alex flopped onto his back. "The library," he moaned. "We can't get there till tomorrow."

"Come on, Alex." Tina tossed a pillow at him. "It's still better than nothing."

"I've got to get home anyway." Jamal stood up. "Let's meet at my house for breakfast tomorrow. We'll go over to the library and figure out where the kidnapper lives. Then we can call Lieutenant McQuade."

Lieutenant McQuade was the Ghostwriter Team's friend on the police force. He knew all the members of the team, and he tried to help them out in any way he could. They'd helped him solve a lot of cases too.

But Alex felt a personal interest in this case. He didn't want to turn it over to the police. "Lieutenant

McQuade? Dream on!" he said, sitting up. "I'm going straight to the kidnapper's house."

"What are you, nuts?" Lenni screeched. "There's an international hunt going on for this kidnapper. Why would you go to his house without the police?"

"We'll just check out the place," Alex assured her. "We'll pretend we're doing a newspaper story about the kidnapping. And if we happen to find Emory Rex . . ." He shrugged. "Then I guess we'll finally get to meet him!"

"I don't know about that," Jamal said. "I still think we should call the police."

"I think Alex is right," Tina said. "Until we have real evidence, we shouldn't bother the police. We'll just go check it out."

"Let's decide about it tomorrow," Hector said as he headed for the door. "I'm with Alex and Tina, though. It can't hurt to look."

"Just think, we could be face to face with Emory Rex by tomorrow afternoon," Tina said.

"Yeah, we could," Alex added, walking out the door behind her. "I just hope his face is still attached to the rest of him."

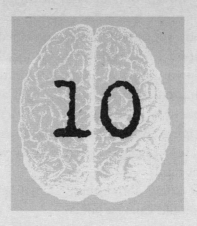

10

At noon the next day, Tina, Alex, and Hector stepped off the elevated subway platform at Coney Island. The team had started their day at the library near their home in Fort Greene, where they found the map of Brooklyn. They had agreed the clues all pointed to Coney Island—there were dolphins at the aquarium there and *coney* was another word for rabbit. When they looked up the addresses of their two remaining suspects, it turned out that Sylvia Owen lived in a neighborhood far from Coney Island. But Frank Bowman's address was right in the middle of Coney Island. They decided he was the prime suspect.

Jamal and Lenni had stayed at the library to see what else they could dig up about Bowman. Hector, Alex, and Tina wanted to check out his house.

And now here they were in Coney Island. On one

side of the subway tracks, seagulls squawked over-
head and the wide beach stretched as far as the eye
could see. It didn't seem like a part of New York
City. But on the other side, tall apartment buildings
were crowded together, just the way they were everywhere else in the city. It was a strange place, but it
made them feel excited.

They weren't sure exactly where Frank Bowman's
house was. According to the map, it was near Astro-
land, the amusement park. But they hadn't been able
to get an exact fix on it because there was no house
number listed in the phone book.

"Well, I guess we should walk down to Fifteenth
Street," Alex said, leading the way down Surf Avenue, away from the subway. Surf Avenue was the
main street in Coney Island. It was filled with a million sights, smells, and sounds. The amusement
park, which was to their left, had dozens of brightly
colored rides, with loud music blaring from each
one. On their right were a lot of little shops, mostly
selling old furniture, portraits of Elvis Presley
painted on black velvet, strange lamps that looked as
if they came from an old episode of *Star Trek,* and
hundreds of little knickknacks. It was hard to tell
which things might be antiques and which should
be tossed in a Dumpster. But just about everything
seemed to be for sale, including a giant old porcelain
kitchen sink.

There were lots of places to get food—from bur-
ritos to corn on the cob to hamburgers and fat, tasty-
looking french fries. And there were game arcades

everywhere. Some of them had modern video games, but there were also old Skee-ball and Whack-a-mole games.

"You know, I came here once with my parents," Tina said. "I think there's a boardwalk that runs parallel to the street we're on. We could still walk toward Fifteenth Street, but we'll be right on the beach."

Alex paused. They were on a case—but the beach was tempting. It wouldn't take any longer to walk down the boardwalk. "Okay," he said. "Let's go."

They cut through the amusement park and down to the boardwalk, right next to the beach and the ocean. The breeze smelled like salt water, and instead of feeling heavy and humid, the air was balmy and cool. And the green street signs told them they were getting closer to Fifteenth Street.

Even with the beautiful scene around her, Tina was feeling jumpy and weird. She could hear the sounds of the amusement park—especially the screams of people riding the Cyclone, the oldest roller coaster in America.

She knew the screams were happy screams. People loved getting scared. Tina knew about that—after all, she read Emory Rex to get scared. But right now she wished she hadn't read quite so many of his stories.

The screams echoed in her ears. What if the roller coaster car slipped off of the wooden slats of the Cyclone? What would the screams sound like then, as the passengers flew into the sky and then plummeted to the ground? Would they sound any different? She couldn't help shivering, even in the warm sunlight.

"This is it," Alex announced. "Fifteenth Street." They walked up the street until they hit Bowery. It wasn't even really a street—just a street sign halfway up the block.

"I don't see a house," Hector said in a hushed voice.

They were standing next to an old, overgrown lot. In the middle of the lot was an ancient, abandoned roller coaster. The red sign that said THUNDERBOLT was still dotted with lightbulbs, though most of them were broken.

Across the narrow street, there were a few abandoned one-story buildings, but they were nothing more than shacks with shrubbery growing around them. There didn't seem to be any place where a person could live.

"Well, where does Bowman live?" Alex wondered. "He's listed in the phone book. He's got to be here."

"Wait, look closer," Tina said. "There's some kind of house under the roller coaster."

"Oh, man. You're right!" Hector said. "But nobody could really be living there."

"Oh, yeah?" Alex said. He pushed his way through a hole in the chain-link fence and started walking through the tall grass toward the house.

"Alex, wait!" Tina said, pushing through after him.

"I found the front door," Alex called back. Tina ran to catch up with him.

"It's not really in bad shape," Alex said. "It's just the outside that looks damaged."

He stepped up to the glass and metal door and peered in. It was dark inside, and Alex couldn't see much. He knocked on the door confidently. Then he jumped back as two huge German shepherds leaped up, barking wildly. They hit their noses against the glass, trying to get out of the door.

"Nice doggies," Alex said in a shaky voice. He looked sidelong at Tina, stepping slowly back from the door. "I guess sneaking in would have been a bad idea," he said.

"I think knocking was a bad idea too," Tina said, looking nervously at the ferocious dogs.

Suddenly the two dogs stopped barking. They still glared at Alex, but they sat quietly. A figure appeared in the doorway.

"All right, Alex. Is that your vicious kidnapper?" Tina asked.

The man in the doorway looked like Mister Rogers. He wore a light blue cardigan sweater and had a little gray mustache. He was smoking a pipe and holding a chipped teacup in his hand. He peered at Alex, Tina, and Hector through thick granny glasses with a scowl on his face.

"What do you want?" he said through the door, sounding annoyed.

"Are you Frank Bowman?" Alex asked.

"Yes, I am," the man said, puffing on his pipe.

"And who might you be? I don't suppose you're selling Girl Scout cookies, unless things have really changed since my youth."

"I'm not a Girl Scout!" Hector said.

"We wanted to ask you about an old friend of yours," Alex said.

"I don't have any old friends," Bowman said grumpily.

"Well, an old acquaintance, then," Alex said. "We thought you might know something about Emory Rex."

Bowman was silent. He puffed on his pipe a few times. "I saw the reports about him on my television," he said. "What makes you think I know anything about a man who vanished?"

"That depends. *Do* you know anything?" Alex asked flatly.

"Who wants to know?" Bowman said. "You don't look like police officers or FBI agents to me. Why should I let this ragtag bunch of children into my home?"

"We're not a ragtag bunch of children," Hector said. "We're a team, and we solve mysteries."

"Oh! A few young Encyclopedia Browns," Bowman said sarcastically. "Well, why don't you go to the Caribbean like the rest of the crime-fighters? I understand that's where they've traced your precious Emory Rex."

"Because we think he's right here, in your house," Alex retorted. "We think *you* kidnapped Emory Rex!"

"Alex!" Tina grabbed his arm, trying to get him to shut up. But Alex was getting really hot under the collar.

"You think I *what?*" The man's eyes widened, and he stepped closer to the door. The dogs growled.

"He didn't mean that!" Tina peeped, stepping in front of Alex. *Is Alex nuts?* she thought. *This guy could be dangerous!*

"I did mean it!" Alex said. "You were jealous of Rex because he went on to be totally famous and you didn't. So you kidnapped him. But we're on to you, Frank Bowman. You'd better let him go."

"I'm really sorry," Tina said. "Alex, if you don't shut up, I'm going to—"

"Don't apologize," Bowman said in a quiet voice. He opened the door and actually gave a little chuckle. "Come on in, why don't you?"

"No thanks," Alex said, planting his hands firmly on his hips. "You can just send Emory Rex out now."

"My dear young man, don't be ridiculous," Bowman said. "Emory Rex isn't in here. I haven't seen him in twenty years! I apologize for teasing you as I did. I don't blame you for getting angry at me. Why don't you come on in, and I'll show you that he's not here."

Alex just stood there, glaring at Bowman. "For heaven's sake," Bowman sighed. "If you're worried that I'll kidnap you, too, leave your young friend out here to keep watch."

Tina turned around to where Hector was standing, looking lost and scared. "You stay out here," she said, and he relaxed noticeably. "You can call the police if we're not out in ten minutes. Alex, come on. We're going inside."

The dogs gave another warning growl as Tina and Alex walked past them, but Bowman just shushed them. "Michael. Wendy. Mind your manners!" he commanded.

"I should have told you the same thing," Tina whispered to Alex as they walked down a short, narrow corridor to a small kitchen.

"I was sure it was him," Alex whispered back. "It seemed so clear at the time. And he got me so angry, with his snotty attitude. But now I'm not so sure." He looked around. "I can't see where he'd hide Rex, anyway."

"That's an excellent point, and one you should have thought of before you knocked on my door," Bowman said, his back to Alex and Tina.

They looked at each other in surprise. "Yes, I heard you," Bowman continued "I may be half blind, but I'm certainly not deaf. Would you care for some tea?" They shook their heads. He led them through the kitchen to another room, where a sofa and two worn chairs stood. He settled into one of the chairs.

"So you think I had something to do with Emory's disappearance," he said. "Well, you're not the only ones. The FBI was here too. And so was a hard-working young newspaper reporter. With very strange hair," he added thoughtfully.

"I'll bet that was Jimmy Clay," Alex said to Tina.

"Jimmy. Yes, I suppose that was his name," Bowman said. "Well, I didn't have much of anything to tell either of them. As I said, I haven't seen Emory in years. And although I was angry when he first broke with me, I don't really care about his fame anymore. From what I understand, he doesn't enjoy it very much anyway."

"He's kind of a loner," Tina said.

"Yes. Something we still have in common," Bowman said. "Anyway, I don't write novels anymore. I have a new passion to write about."

"What's that?" Alex asked. "True crime? Comic books?"

"Gardening," Bowman answered.

"Gardening?" Alex couldn't believe it. "Come on. You gave up horror so you could write about flowers?"

"Sort of," Bowman said. He sat up in his chair. "Take a look at the plant on the table to your right."

Alex looked at the plant. It didn't look like any kind of flower he'd ever seen. It had two wide, flat leaves. It almost seemed to have teeth at the edges of the leaves. "What is that?" he asked.

"A Venus flytrap," Bowman said. "Her name is Esmerelda. She is my pride and my joy. Would you like to see me feed her?"

"You mean *water* her, right?" Alex asked.

"No, he means feed her," Tina said. "I've never seen one up close. Can I watch?" she asked.

Alex's jaw dropped almost to the floor as Bowman

opened a green plastic ant farm and picked out a single ant with a pair of tweezers. The ant struggled in the metal grip, but Bowman held it firmly. He walked back across the room and placed the squirming insect in the center of the two wide leaves.

Immediately the leaves slammed shut. The ant was toast.

"That plant didn't *eat* that bug, did it?" Alex squeaked.

"Oh, yes. My little Esmerelda has quite an appetite," Bowman said admiringly. Alex stepped back from the plant and put one hand on his neck.

"How long will it take to digest?" Tina asked admiringly, peering at the plant from all sides.

"Oh, it's a matter of days," Bowman answered. "Can I show you two the rest of the house? Just so you understand that Emory Rex isn't bound and gagged in any of my spare rooms."

"I'd love to see your garden," Tina said. "I guess the house itself goes in a circle, and the garden is in the middle?"

"Yes, sort of like a courtyard," Bowman said, as he led them through the house. It circled around the roller coaster. Each room led into the next. The rooms were small and cramped. Once they had gone all the way around, Bowman put his hand on the bolt of a large wooden door.

"Well?" he said. "Can I show you my garden?"

"Uh—no thanks," Alex said.

"Alex, come on," Tina said. "You were so gung-ho when we walked in here. The least we can do is look at his garden."

"Are you nuts?" Alex asked. "Did you see that bug-eating plant? Who knows how big those things can get?"

Tina rolled her eyes. "You are really silly sometimes," she said. She walked through the door into the garden.

Alex screwed up his courage. He knew he had to walk through that door—but he wasn't sure what he was going to find. Half of him still thought he was going to see Emory Rex, gagged and tied up with vines of ivy. The other half of him was positive he was about to feel the massive jaws of a kid-eating Venus flytrap.

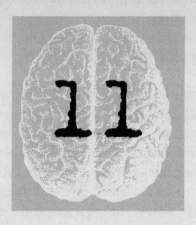

Alex felt himself break into a cold sweat as he stepped out the door. But on the other side was nothing more than a garden—although it was the greenest, lushest garden Alex had ever seen.

A glass roof stretched across the courtyard, transforming it into a greenhouse. A fine mist of water hung in the air. It was like being in the middle of a rain forest. There were plants with wide leaves and bright flowers everywhere. A gray stone path led up and down the rows of plants.

"This is the biggest collection of this strain of orchid in the world," Bowman announced as he led Alex and Tina through the garden. "My writings on these plants are well known. Just a few months ago I published a new reference book about them, and it has already become an important part of every serious gardener's library." He spoke proudly. "I don't think Emory Rex has ever done anything like that, do you?"

"Probably not," Alex admitted. "I don't think he writes a lot of reference books."

"Or gardening books," Tina added.

Bowman smiled at his flower collection, lost in thought. He gave a deep, happy sigh. Finally he looked at Alex and Tina again.

"Well! We've been through every room in the house. There is no basement, and you've seen every corner of my secret garden. Did you two spot a desperate kidnapped writer anywhere?"

"No, we didn't," Alex admitted glumly.

"Then perhaps you should return to your friend, so that he doesn't get worried," Bowman said, leading them out of the garden and into the hallway of the house. The dogs were still sitting there, and they raised their heads curiously as Alex and Tina walked past.

"Thank you for your visit," Bowman said, opening the front door.

"Mr. Bowman, wait," Tina said, stopping in the doorway. "There's still something I want to ask you."

"And what might that be, my dear?" Bowman asked.

"Why did you stop working with Rex? Why did you guys have that big fight where he kicked you out of the partnership?"

Bowman's face got very sad. The lines in his forehead deepened, and he pursed his lips thoughtfully.

"Well, of course I can't speak for Emory myself. He's the only one who could really answer that question. But from what I can tell, from thinking about it for the past twenty years . . ." He shook his head. "I suppose Emory was just very young, and very easily convinced. And when various people told him he could do just as well without me, he believed them."

He cocked an eyebrow and shrugged. "Perhaps they were right," he added. "He has done quite well, hasn't he?"

Tina was sorry she had made him go through his bad memories. "I suppose," she said. "But I'll bet his stories would have been even better with your help."

"Yeah. You guys might have written about a giant Venus flytrap," Alex said.

Bowman threw his head back and gave a long laugh. "Perhaps you're right, my boy," he said as the dogs thumped their tails on the ground.

"Thanks for showing us your house," Alex said. "And I'm sorry I accused you of kidnapping."

"It was no bother," Bowman said. "Come back whenever you wish. It's not every day I'm connected with an international manhunt!"

Alex and Tina walked out of the lot to where Hector was waiting anxiously.

"So what happened?" he asked. "Was Emory Rex in there?"

"No, he wasn't there," Alex said, looking discouraged. "I just don't get it. All the clues led right here, to Coney Island. We should have found him right here. But all we found were some creepy plants and an old guy."

"Alex, don't give up," Tina begged. "There has to be someplace else we can look. Some more clues."

"I know one place where *I* want to look," Hector announced.

They turned and looked at him. He was holding the casebook open in his hands. "And we even have the address right here. I still think she had something to do with it."

"Who?" Alex wanted to know.

"The fan club lady. You know, Sylvia Owen. She lives in Brooklyn too."

"How is she going to kidnap someone?" Tina asked.

"I don't know. But as long as there's more investigating we can do, we should do it."

Alex looked over Hector's shoulder at the casebook. "Nobody knows Rex's books like she does, that's for sure," he said.

"Right," Tina said. "So if there's anything in the notes that we missed, she'll be able to point them out."

"And if she knows anything about his disappearance, we might be able to get it out of her," Alex added. "Hector, you're a genius!"

"Thank you, thank you," Hector congratulated himself, bowing to an imaginary audience. "I'm glad you finally appreciate my true abilities."

• • •

It took about forty minutes to get to Sylvia's neighborhood by subway. By that time it was the middle of the afternoon.

Hector, Tina, and Alex knew the area pretty well. It wasn't far from Fort Greene, and the main branch of the Brooklyn Public Library was there, as well as Prospect Park, where there was a zoo and a lake with paddleboats.

But they didn't know the streets that well. They had to walk back and forth along the edge of the park a few times before they found President Street. Minutes later, they found Sylvia's address, number 802.

"Here it is," Hector announced.

Number 802 President Street was a large apartment building with a wide, fancy lobby and an awning stretching out to the sidewalk. A doorman, whose job it was to greet all visitors, stepped out of the doorway and smiled at Alex, Tina, and Hector.

"Can I help you?" he asked.

"We're here to see Sylvia Owen," Tina answered.

"Sylvia Owen? I don't know," he said doubtfully.

"She's not expecting us," Alex admitted. "But I think she'll be glad to see us. We met her at a convention."

The doorman shook his head. "Poor Ms. Owen, she doesn't want to see anybody," he said. "That convention was very, very bad for her. She's been very sad since she came back."

"Please. Can't we just talk to her for a second?" Tina pleaded.

The doorman sighed and knocked on one of the apartment doors that opened onto the lobby. It opened a small crack, and he murmured something to the person inside. Alex could just make out Sylvia's outline. She was shaking her head.

"Please, Ms. Owen," Alex begged. "We just wanted to talk about Emory Rex."

"We're trying to find him. We need your help!" Tina added.

Sylvia paused for a moment. Then she stepped back from the door and opened it. "Thank you, Stavros," she said in a low voice. "Come on in," she said to the kids.

Alex couldn't believe that the woman in the doorway was the same Sylvia Owen that he had met at the convention. She had been creepy, sure, but she had also been enthusiastic and happy. This woman looked totally miserable. Her skin was sallow, and she looked as if she hadn't bothered to eat much in the past few days. Her hair wasn't frizzy anymore. It hung limp and greasy around her face as if it were sad too.

They followed her into a foyer, where they came face to face with an angry cat. Alex leaped back in alarm, thinking it wasn't his day for animals.

Then he looked again.

The cat was stuffed. Its yellow eyes were made of glass, and it was stuck in that angry position forever.

"Oh, don't mind Fifi," Sylvia said with a wave of her hand. "She was one of my early projects. I just couldn't stand to let her go when she died."

Alex, Tina, and Hector squeezed against the wall of the narrow hallway and walked past the stuffed cat. They came into the living room.

A strange scent that was hard to identify hung in the air. It was sweet, but there was something rotten about it too. The room was the most overcrowded space the kids had ever been in. The couch and chairs were huge and bulky, covered with wild floral prints. An entire wall was taken up by a white bookshelf, where every Emory Rex book was displayed in its own plastic case. The television blared in the corner, tuned to the all-news cable channel.

"I'm hoping to catch any kind of special report," Sylvia explained, waving her hand toward the television. "You never know when there might be a break in the case. I've been so horribly worried about Emory."

"We have too," Tina said. "We were at the convention. Do you remember us?"

Sylvia studied their faces for a moment. She nodded slowly. "Well, yes, I suppose I do," she said. "We rode the subway together, didn't we? And then you stopped off at my table."

"That's right." Alex nodded.

"But this one wasn't with you then," she added, pointing at Hector. "Were you?"

Hector shook his head. He stuck close to Alex and didn't say a word.

"Whatsa matter, cat got your tongue?" Sylvia asked. Hector looked behind him at the cat in the foyer and pressed his lips together tightly.

"Oh! Where are my manners?" Sylvia said with a start. "I'm so preoccupied with Emory, I forgot to offer you any refreshments. Would you like some lemonade? It's a hot, hot day," she said.

"No thanks," Tina said. "We were just hoping you could—"

"Well, I've got to have some," Sylvia said, walking back toward the other end of the apartment. "You kids come along. I'm sure we can find something you'll like back here. And you can see my collection."

Alex, Tina, and Hector followed Sylvia through her apartment. It made Bowman's house look normal.

They had to walk down a narrow hallway, past several rooms, to get to the kitchen. They couldn't help peeking in the open doors of each room. In the first room the walls were painted a deep blue—not the kind of color anyone would normally paint a room. The dark color made the tiny room look even smaller. Along one wall was a mural of the ocean, stretching out toward the horizon. A bright, hot sun was painted in the sky. On the other side of the room, a huge wooden steering wheel from a ship was set up on a stand. A stuffed parrot was perched on the wheel, its beak open as if it were calling out.

"Land ho," Tina whispered.

"Say what?" Hector asked.

"That's what the parrot keeps saying," Alex explained. "This crew is lost at sea, totally adrift. Their

106

sails were destroyed in a big storm and the wind won't blow anyway. They're slowly running out of food and water, and the parrot keeps yelling, 'Land Ho! Land Ho,' even though there's no land in sight."

"They can't catch the bird to shut it up so they all go crazy," Tina continued.

"Let me guess. This is an Emory Rex story?" Hector asked.

"You got it," Alex told him. " 'Madness on the High Seas.' "

"Though most people just call it 'Land Ho,' " Tina added.

The room across the hall was decorated like another Emory Rex book. The walls were painted to look like a city park. Instead of a couch, there was a park bench. And all over the room were stuffed squirrels, balanced on their hind legs. They were all staring at the park bench. There had to be two dozen of them.

"Yeech," Tina said, shivering. " 'The Massacre.' "

"More Emory Rex?" Hector asked.

"Uh-huh," Alex said.

The next room, farther down the hall, was even more bizarre. It had a normal bookshelf and chair. But on the chair, a male dummy was leaning back with its arms and legs flailing out. A realistic-looking stomach was punching its way out of the dummy's middle.

"The dummy's fake, but the stomach is real," Sylvia called back, seeing that Tina, Alex, and Hector were standing in the doorway of that room. "Pig's stomach. Got it from the butcher shop and figured out how to stuff it. Pretty good, huh?"

Tina gagged. The sickly-sweet smell, plus the disgusting images that decorated the rooms, made her want to throw up. Alex grabbed her arm and steered her the rest of the way into the kitchen.

That's where she figured out what the sweet, rotten smell was. Sylvia had dried flowers hanging from the ceiling, like bright-colored corpses. Petals of dozens of other flowers were gathered in bowls all over the place. The smell of the dead flowers was overpowering.

"Your apartment is really . . . interesting," Alex said. Tina sat on a stool at the kitchen table.

"I wish I had a bigger place," Sylvia sighed as she poured herself some lemonade and arranged cookies on a plate. "I'd love to have a different room for every book and short story Emory Rex wrote. As it is, I had to pick my favorites." She stopped talking abruptly and put down the cookie she was holding. "Oh, Emory," she sniffled as a tear escaped down her cheek. "I hope you're all right."

Hector walked over to Sylvia and put a hand on her arm. "I'm sure somebody's going to find him soon," he assured her. "Don't be scared."

"You're such a sweet child," she sighed, patting Hector's hand. "But I'm sure there's nothing that people like us can do to help a man like Emory."

"Sure there is!" Hector exclaimed. "We're going

to help find him ourselves. We've solved lots of mysteries. We've even got a casebook."

"A casebook?" Sylvia looked curious. "What do you mean?"

"It's where we write down everything when we're working on a case," Tina explained. She was feeling better, now that there was something beside stuffed pigs' stomachs to think about. "We make a notebook with all the suspects, clues, and evidence. You want to see?"

Tina was pleased to see how Sylvia perked up at the news that someone else cared about the disappearance of Emory Rex. Tina pulled out the casebook and flipped it open.

"Wait. Hang on a second," Alex said. But he was too late.

Sylvia's eyes widened. She pointed at the suspects page.

"But that's—that's *my* name!" she cried out.

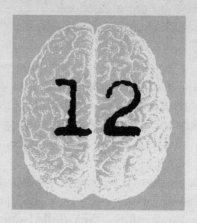

12

Tina gulped. She expected Sylvia to twist her lips into a frown and yell at them in a fury. How could she have been so stupid? Why would she ever show a casebook to someone outside the team, anyway? She squeezed her eyes shut and waited for the screaming to start.

Instead she heard laughter.

"Oh, you kids!" Sylvia roared, holding her sides as she guffawed. "Did you think I had something to do with Emory's disappearance? Oh, you are too much!"

Alex let out a long, slow breath of air. "Then you're not mad?" he asked.

"Mad? Oh, honey!" Sylvia gave another series of giggles, then a snorting breath. "No, I'm not mad. I'm flattered!" She shook her head, looking at the list. "I'm glad you kiddies are so thorough. Checking out every avenue," she said.

"We always try to follow every lead," Tina said.

"And it's nice to be in such good company," Sylvia went on, running her finger down the page. "Good old Frank Bowman. He's a sweet old thing. I wonder what ever became of him?"

"He's living in Coney Island," Alex told her. "We went to see him before we came to see you."

"Do you know him?" Tina asked.

"Well, I met him once. Seventeen years ago, when I was just starting this fan club business. I wanted to get to know absolutely everyone who had ever known Emory Rex. I found out about that first book deal, and I tracked down Frank and bought him lunch. He didn't say much about Emory, though. And I had to keep shouting to be heard."

"Why? Was the restaurant loud?" Hector asked.

"Loud? Oh, no." Sylvia smiled at the memory. "No, that stubborn mule hadn't changed the batteries in his hearing aid," she explained.

Tina and Alex exchanged confused looks. "Hearing aid?" Tina said.

"Did he wear glasses, too?" Alex asked carefully.

"Glasses? Heavens, no. That man had perfect twenty-twenty vision," Sylvia said. "Eyes like a hawk. I remember he talked a lot about bird-watching, and how his eyes were so much more dependable than his ears. No, it was Emory who wore the glasses." She sighed. "It's just one more thing I have in common with him."

Her words seemed to sit in a cloud over the heads of Alex, Tina, and Hector. They knew that things were not as they seemed. They couldn't quite piece it together yet, but . . .

"We've got to get back to our friends," Tina said. "Thanks for the cookies." She stood up and clutched the casebook to her chest.

"Yeah. And the great stories," Alex added. He was already edging toward the door.

"You're going so soon!" Sylvia said. "What's your rush?"

"We promised to meet our friends by four," Tina explained. "We've really got to go. But I promise, we'll come back to visit you soon."

"I'll be having a party when they track down Emory," Sylvia told them as she followed them through the house to the front door. "You'd better come back for that, huh?"

"Oh, you bet," Alex called over his shoulder as they scrambled out the door. They waved goodbye to the doorman and raced up to the corner of the park.

"Hearing aid?" Tina gasped. "No glasses? That doesn't sound like the Frank Bowman we met."

"I don't know what it all means," Alex said. "We've got to get the rest of the team together."

•   •   •

On the subway ride home, they called a rally at Tina's house. They also added a note to the evidence section of the casebook:

Sylvia Owen said that Frank Bowman did not wear glasses and that he was hard of hearing. But when we met him, he was wearing thick glasses and no hearing aid, and he heard every word we said.

When they got off the train and began running up the street toward Tina's house, they could see Jamal and Lenni already sitting on the stoop.

"Well? What's going on?" Lenni asked as Tina led the way into the house.

"We expected to hear from you a lot earlier," Jamal said. "Your whole trip out to Coney Island was wasted."

"What are you talking about?" Alex asked.

"Lenni and I were looking through some old magazines and newspapers," Jamal explained. "And we found out that Frank Bowman couldn't be living there anymore."

"But his name was listed in the phone book," Tina pointed out.

"It must have been an old listing," Jamal said. "We ran a computer search for any mention of Frank Bowman in any newspaper. We only found one article—in a small local paper, from almost fifteen years ago."

"So? What does that prove?" Alex asked.

"It was an *obituary*," Lenni said. "Frank Bowman's been dead for fifteen years!"

There was a stunned silence.

"Wait a minute. Dead?" Alex asked.

"This just gets weirder and weirder," Hector murmured.

"Pretty frustrating, huh?" Jamal said. "I'll bet you were pretty mad when you got all the way out to Coney Island and found out that Bowman wasn't there."

"But that's just the thing," Tina said. "He was there. We talked to him!"

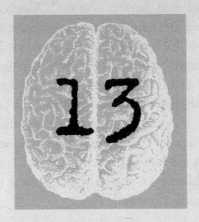

"Did we see a ghost when we met Frank Bowman?" Hector asked. His eyes were almost popping out of his head. "Wouldn't Ghostwriter have noticed if we were talking to another ghost?"

Alex looked at Tina. "I don't think we saw Frank Bowman's ghost today," he said.

She shook her head. "No. I think we saw Emory Rex."

The rest of the team heard what Tina said and turned slowly to look at her.

"Um, excuse me?" Lenni asked.

"It's the only explanation that makes sense," Tina said. "All the clues pointed to Coney Island. So we know Emory Rex had to be there somewhere. Frank Bowman's house was there, so we figured out that he had to be the kidnapper. But all the physical evidence says that we didn't see Frank Bowman at all."

"According to Sylvia Owen, Bowman could hardly hear and had perfect vision," Alex continued. "The guy we met could hear fine—but he wore thick glasses. Just like Emory Rex. It had to be him."

"You mean he staged his own disappearance?" Lenni said, shaking her head. "That is so totally nuts! Why would anybody do something that crazy?"

"Maybe it's not so nuts," Jamal said. "Think about it. Alex and Tina said that Rex almost got trampled by his fans at that convention. And he hates publicity. Maybe he wanted to disappear under the name of Frank Bowman."

"It's still weird," Lenni said, shaking her head. "But let's say that Emory Rex is Frank Bowman, just for argument's sake. That still leaves one really big question."

"What's that?" Alex asked.

"Why did he disappear from the convention like that?" Lenni said.

Alex stood up. "There's only one way to find out," he declared.

There were still a few hours of light left when they got off the subway at Coney Island. This was the second time in one day that Alex, Tina, and Hector had made this trip. But Jamal and Lenni were doing it for the first time that day.

"Don't you think we should call Lieutenant McQuade?" Jamal asked as they approached the Thunderbolt.

"Yeah, I'm still not convinced that confronting Rex is the best idea in the world," Lenni added.

Tina shook her head. "If it was so important for Emory Rex to remain anonymous, we have to respect that."

"But there's a total FBI manhunt going on!" Lenni pointed out. "We could be obstructing justice or something."

"He deserves a chance to explain himself," Tina said firmly.

She and Alex stood in front of the rickety door again. This time the dogs just looked at them. Before they could knock, Frank Bowman appeared in the doorway. He stared at them through the glass with a grave expression.

He finally opened the door. "Well," he said. "I suppose you have more questions for me. And there are more of you," he added, taking in the rest of the team. "Come on in."

He led them straight through to the garden, where they sat on a wooden bench and on a few large stones.

"And how can I help you children today?" Frank Bowman said, standing by a tall sunflower. "Would you like to accuse me of stealing the Hope Diamond? Or perhaps you think I'm responsible for the extinction of the dinosaurs?"

"No, we don't think any of those things," Tina said.

"We think you're Emory Rex," Alex said.

Frank Bowman just looked at Alex. He had no

expression on his face at all: He wasn't smiling, and he wasn't frowning. He was just looking.

"I had a feeling you were going to say that," Frank Bowman finally said. Then he gave a long sigh. "Well, you're right. I am Emory Rex."

"I knew it!" Alex said, standing up. "I knew Emory Rex was here, in this house, in Coney Island. I just didn't know that *you* were the one—the man who vanished!"

"Why did you do it?" Tina asked. "Why were you pretending to be Frank Bowman? And why did you disappear from the convention like that?"

Emory Rex shook his head and didn't say anything for a long time. He looked up at the glass roof and squinted, then looked back down at the ground.

Tina stood up and put a hand on his arm. "Were you afraid that the fans wouldn't like the end of *Murdernet*?"

"Wouldn't like it?" Emory chuckled and shook his head. "My dear girl, they wouldn't have liked it or hated it. It doesn't exist!"

"Doesn't exist?" Alex was stunned. "You mean you didn't write it?"

"I mean I *couldn't* write it," Emory said. "I don't expect you kids to understand. You see, I was always a writer. It was just something I had to do. When I was a young man, I would wake up at five in the morning so that I could write for two hours before I went to work. It wasn't always easy, but it made me feel complete. It was my dream to be a great writer."

"What about Frank Bowman?" Hector asked. "Wasn't he your partner?"

"Poor, dear Frank," Emory said, shaking his head. "We went to high school and college together. All along, we encouraged each other to write. We thought it would be a great experience to work together. But once we got the contract, the words suddenly deserted Frank. He just couldn't write anymore."

"So you dumped him," Lenni grumbled.

"So I dumped him," Emory admitted. "I was young and full of dreams. I was foolish. Never thinking of his feelings, of the encouragement I could give him, I allowed my publisher to push Frank out of the project. We never spoke again."

"Until he died?" Jamal asked.

"Correct again," Emory said. "Technically, we didn't speak even then. Bowman knew he was dying for months. He wrote me a long letter telling me that he forgave me, that he had found peace here, with his plants and flowers. And he asked me to take care of them. He left his precious garden to me." He shook his head, overcome with emotion. "I stabbed him in the back, and he still gave me the greatest gift. He gave me anonymity."

Hector tugged on Lenni's sleeve. "Anemone?" he whispered.

"Anonymity," Lenni explained quietly. "He means that he could be anonymous here. Nobody knew who he was."

"I hushed up the news of Bowman's death,"

Emory went on. "It wasn't announced in his gardening journals or in any major paper. I had excellent publishing contacts. Slowly I withdrew from my city life and began hiding here, in the garden. I continued to publish my books. And I also managed to finish a few of Bowman's old manuscripts and publish them under his name. But for the past few years, it has given me no joy."

"You don't like to write anymore?" Tina asked.

"I saw that my fans, as they are called, seemed to care less and less about me. Because they read Rex books, they thought they knew Rex. But they didn't understand *me* at all. And when the time came to finish this book—well, the words stopped coming to me, too."

"But Myra Manning had already announced that you were going to appear at the convention," Tina said.

"Yes. She did that with my permission," Emory responded. "I told her that I wanted to surprise everyone—including Century Books—with the ending. I thought that the deadline would encourage me to write. But I just couldn't do it."

"I went to the convention, hoping for a miracle," he continued. "I thought I might admit my problem to the fans directly. But when they swarmed over me before the speaking engagement . . . I got scared. I thought they would rise up and devour me!"

"Mr. Rex, come on," Lenni said. "I mean, no offense, but this is reality, not one of your books. The people weren't going to *devour* you!"

Emory shrugged. "Well, they might have booed," he said. "Rather than face them, I snuck out of the backstage area just before the curtain opened. I dropped my name tag in a garbage can and allowed myself to be escorted out by the security guards, who did not appreciate anonymous guests at their convention. And I've been hiding out here ever since."

"But how could you think that we wouldn't care? Don't you see what's been happening since you disappeared?" Tina asked. "Mr. Rex, the FBI is in the Caribbean looking for you. We visited your fan club president, and she's crying about you. And our team has been trying to track you down. Do you think we would have done that if we didn't care?"

Emory Rex smiled at Tina. "That is kind of you," he said. "It was kind of all of you to come here. But I think perhaps the words have left me for good."

There didn't seem to be anything left to say. Emory Rex insisted he wanted to stay hidden and he couldn't write anymore. The Ghostwriter Team said good-bye, slowly filed out of the house, and walked glumly to the subway station.

"I'm getting sick of Coney Island," Hector complained.

"I'm getting sick of you," Lenni snapped.

They were all feeling awful about Emory Rex. They dropped their tokens into the turnstile in silence and boarded the train, which was waiting in the station.

"I guess we should call Lieutenant McQuade," Alex murmured.

"I suppose," Tina agreed. "Just so people don't keep flying all over the world looking for Rex."

"Our poor casebook," Lenni said, flipping it open. "We solved the mystery, but we didn't help Emory Rex."

Alex took the casebook and looked at the two weird notes—the clues that had led them to the famous author's home. The keys to the whole puzzle.

"That's strange," he said.

"What?" Tina asked.

"I was just thinking. If Emory Rex really didn't want to be found . . . why did he send those notes?"

Now everyone was looking at the paragraphs on the page.

"Yeah, that is weird," Lenni agreed. "Why would anyone become totally anonymous, then stage his own disappearance, and then send hints to everyone who's looking for him? It doesn't make sense."

"It does make sense . . . if he *wanted* to be found!" Tina said with a gasp.

"If he wanted to be found?" Jamal asked. "Then why disappear?"

"Maybe he thought nobody cared," Tina said. "He disappeared and sent out the clues just in case there was someone, somewhere, who cared enough to come find him. It was a huge test!"

"Maybe he needed us to come find him," Alex added. "To prove that there were people that understood him. Although I have to say, he sure didn't *look* like he felt much better."

As if in answer to their realization, Ghostwriter began buzzing around the casebook.

"What's Ghostwriter doing?" Lenni asked. "He couldn't have heard us. And we didn't write any of that down."

Slowly at first, then more and more quickly, Ghostwriter began picking letters off the page and fitting them together. When he needed more letters, he grabbed them off of the advertisements above their heads in the subway car. Words were reeling across the top of the page in the casebook at break-neck speed.

Nobody knew that computer like Moseby. He had created it with his own mind, with his own imagination. And he could destroy it, too.

He strapped on the virtual-reality helmet and glove and, in an instant, he created his own ultimate weapon. A weapon that would save Janet . . . and destroy the demon machine for-ever!

"Moseby? Janet?" Tina squealed. "It must be the end of the book. It's the end of *Murdernet!*"

"Rex must be writing it now!" Alex cheered. "We

did it. We found him . . . and we found the end of the book!"

They sat in rapt silence as they watched the words spill across the page.

Emory Rex was back in business.

14
Epilogue

"Get your ice-cold eyeballs! Ice-cold eyeballs, worm sandwiches, I got 'em right here!"

"Hey! I'll have one of those," Alex called out.

Slim Haut stopped her cart. "Okay. Do you want blue, brown, green, or hazel?"

Alex turned to Tina. "Green?"

Tina nodded. "It looks like pistachio," she said, grinning.

Alex handed over the money and picked up the round, shiny ice-cream ball.

"Ugh! Are you guys actually going to eat that?" Lenni asked. She was totally disgusted.

"Oh, yeah!" Tina said, licking the eyeball and then handing it back to Alex. "Everybody who goes to horror conventions eats them."

It was a month later. Century Books had arranged

for a second horror convention to be held, since the first one had been such a bust. The summer was coming to an end, though it was still sweltering outside. But inside the hotel in midtown Manhattan, it was air-conditioner fresh. The Ghostwriter Team was definitely excited to be there—especially Gaby and Casey, who were back from camp.

"Come on, it looks like most of the people have already gone into the auditorium," Casey said, trying to push her friends toward the door.

"We're in no hurry," Alex said confidently. But he strolled to the door anyway.

Most of the room was already filled, but seven seats in the front row had a bright green ribbon tied across them. Each seat had a name on it—the name of a Ghostwriter Team member.

They got to their seats just as the lights went down. A hush fell over the audience as Myra Manning stepped out from the wings.

"Well! Hello again," she said, and some people in the audience laughed.

"I don't think I need to tell you how exciting this day is," she went on. "In fact, a lot of you probably have heard my speech before. And those of you who didn't have certainly heard about Emory Rex on the news. Well, we were lucky enough to grab a moment of his time, even though he's already hard at work on his next novel, *Venus Mantrap*. So without further ado, I'd like to present to you . . . Emory Rex!"

She pulled the golden cord, and the curtains swished open.

This time, Emory Rex was seated in the chair. He looked up and smiled at the audience through his thick glasses, and everyone went wild, cheering and clapping for several minutes.

Finally they all settled down, and Emory Rex began to read the final chapter of *Murdernet*. Alex had read the whole thing already, thanks to Ghostwriter.

Now he wanted to enjoy everyone else's reaction. He looked around the room.

Next to him, Sylvia Owen looked radiantly happy as she gazed up at Emory Rex. Alex had talked Emory Rex into giving her an exclusive interview for her fan club newsletter.

Myra Manning was beaming from backstage. The publicity surrounding Rex's disappearance had done wonders for the sales of his books. Her assistant, Barbara Casey, was looking relieved too, although she still seemed a little jumpy.

And Alex was totally satisfied. He and the rest of the team were all going to get personally autographed copies of *Murdernet* as soon as it came out as a book.

Alex had been enjoying daydreaming as Rex read. He drifted back to Rex's story just at the very end, when the evil Dr. Picket's brain-computer was finally blown apart by Moseby and Janet. Alex thought he had heard the ending, but Ghostwriter had left a few details out. Alex had no idea that there was an extra surprise to come.

"My brains, my brains," Dr. Picket wailed, crawling along the floor among the ruins of his computer.

The seven gray blobs looked harmless now. They twitched helplessly on the ground, surrounded by their jellylike juice. It was hard to believe they had once been at the center of a plot to destroy the whole world.

"My darlings!" he sobbed. "My angels. My intrepid Alex, my thoughtful Tina! And little Casey and Hector, the vulnerable youngest." He kissed the brains as they seemed to exhale and die. "Lenni. Jamal. Gaaaabyyyy!"

But the brains were gone. And Picket's plan was ruined.

Alex looked over at the rest of the team. They were all grinning back at him, surprised.

"He put us in!" said Lenni. "We're the brains in the computer!"

"Did he call me the vulnerable youngest?" Casey whispered.

"Don't knock it!" Alex whispered back. Then he leaned back in his chair as a satisfied glow spread through him. Tina was grinning from ear to ear.

She wrote a note to Alex on the back of her place marker: *Did Ghostwriter tell you Mr. Rex used our names?*

In response, the green glow gathered up letters from signs around the room. The letters grew until

they were six feet tall, then danced through the air above Emory Rex's head.

SURPRISE! Ghostwriter said. Then the letters flipped around, and more flew up to the stage.

You guys deserve it. Great work!

Look for the next exciting Ghostwriter book . . .

ALIEN ALERT
by Susan Korman

Aliens have landed on earth!

The Ghostwriter Team is getting frantic messages from a very scared boy who lives in the past. His town has been invaded by huge outer-space aliens that plan to take over the world. Can the team defeat the enormous killer aliens? They need Ghostwriter's help, but traveling into the past is sapping their ghostly friend's strength. If the Ghostwriter Team can't halt the alien attack, will the world come to an end before they're even born?